HERE
LIES

HERE
LIES

A NOVEL

OLIVIA CLARE FRIEDMAN

Grove Press
New York

The poem on page 116 was originally published in *The 26-Hour Day* by Olivia Clare (New Issues Poetry and Prose, 2015).

First Grove Atlantic hardcover edition: March 2022

This book was set in 11.5-pt. Sabon by Alpha Design & Composition of Pittsfield, NH.

Published simultaneously in Canada
Printed in the United States of America

FIRST EDITION

ISBN 978-0-8021-2939-0
eISBN 978-0-8021-4706-6

Grove Press
an imprint of Grove Atlantic
154 West 14th Street
New York, NY 10011

Distributed by Publishers Group West

groveatlantic.com

22 23 24 25   10 9 8 7 6 5 4 3 2 1

for Willa
for Craig
and for Mary Belle

HERE
LIES

BEFORE

From before I began, I loved her. This was what I knew. Before the beginning, before I was born from her, before bones and blood and body, before egg.

My mother, Naomi, was dead and not buried. Dead in fact for half a year. Her body burned to ashes by the state—bones, heart, feet, eyes burned to dust, against her wish, against mine, and that was that. I was trying to understand.

I was at the library for the first time since she'd died. Upstairs, on the second floor, the air was muggy and dim. I zoomed between empty carrels, toward the faraway corner, a place I used to call my own—a row of three computers. Here, I could be alone. No one, not for years, seemed to know the spot. To my right were shelves of hardbacks, amber and green, the color of jewels. To my left, out the smudged picture window, I could watch the sun-sopped field of weeds and goldenrod shake in the wind, feel my own insides shake in an answer.

I walked to the spot, heard my own breathing. I reached the corner and stopped—in front of me, a girl sat at one of the keyboards, hunched and glum. She'd been squinting into the screen when she heard me and glanced up—a burst of hazel-gold eyes, silky blue eye shadow—said nothing, went back to her screen. I said nothing too. How long had she been coming? I wanted to make her get up, shove her chair, force her to leave. That was what the mean-hearted me would do, or the bold-hearted me, and sometimes I allowed my dolty-dolt heart these fantasies. All I wanted was peace. I wanted to do what I needed to do, alone.

I told her to go away in my head. *Get gone, get gone, get gone.* I sat down on the other end, left a computer station between us, logged myself in. The girl clicked and typed, typed and clicked. Her fingernails were painted a clean, frosty blue. She breathed through her mouth, loud puffs of air. She put a foot up on the chair, adjusted a pink, sparkling flip-flop, the kind you see in the drugstore aisle with Water Babies sunscreen and inflatable beach balls. She scratched her naked toes.

"They have computers downstairs," I told her. "Downstairs they go faster."

"Mm-hmm." She looked at her screen.

"These are dinosaurs," I said. "You can't even watch a movie."

I hit the back of the monitor hard, as though it weren't working, as though that would show how feeble it was, but it was working just fine.

"I know that already," she said.

I glimpsed her screen. She was speed-scrolling through pictures and paragraphs of gossip about TV stars and blog celebrities and Hollywood he-said, she-said heartbreaks. She looked younger than me, but near enough to my age, give or take, and I was twenty-two.

I said, "Downstairs, the AC won't blow on you."

"I'm not cold," she said.

I said, "Downstairs, the librarian sneaks you free Cokes."

"I'm not thirsty," she said.

We both knew the first floor's bank of computers was crowded with people watching the news, talking to relatives on video chat, streaming everything from car chases to girl-gone-missing crime shows. She rolled her bottom lip under her front teeth. She brought her lean leg up, focused on the screen. Even doing that, she was graceful. I went to my screen. We sat like that, squinting and pecking. *Get gone, get gone.* I talked in my head. In case she was watching me, I didn't do what I'd gone there to do. Instead I watched a video on mute about glowing jellyfish in the deep sea, another about people at their toilets finding coiled-up snakes. She'd taken the spot by the window with the clear view of the wild field. Sometimes she'd turn, look out to the field, but then she'd turn back to her screen, back to her nothingness, her nothing news, gossipy gunk. She didn't care about the field like I did. I knew the names of things. Sprouting bluets, stray pink lilies, tattered dandelions, Bermuda grass.

The next day it went like that too. Me watching soundless jellyfish and snakes. I came up to the second floor in

3

the afternoon and there she was, with her blue-shadowed lids and a paisley purse she kept under her chair, and there I sat, and scratch-scratch-scratch and scroll-scroll-scroll and peck-peck-peck. She smelled like sweat and damp roses and green tea, like cheap mall perfume I'd bought in high school. She watched videos of baby hippos and skateboard stunts and kittens stealing dog beds. She turned the volume up, laughed to herself, leaned closer to the screen. We stayed that way, not talking, each one lost to the other.

On the third day, I sneaked two icy beers in my purse. The library started its shutdown at four-thirty, dimmed the buzzy fluorescent lights. Pegeen—I'd known Pegeen all my life—called out over the PA, the library was going bye-bye, nighty-night, off to sleep now. That was how Pegeen always said it. I dug deep in my purse, brought out an Abita Purple Haze. They could be hard to get, but I knew a place.

"You want one?" I asked the girl.

She turned to look for the first time that day, a new kind of life flickering in her face.

"Fuck, yes," she said.

I'd meant it as a bribe. *Take this, don't come back tomorrow.* But seeing her that happy for a beer—I decided I wanted the other. I'd drink it quick, talk for a few minutes, ask her to get gone, to stay home tomorrow. No offense, nothing personal, just be gone tomorrow.

We took our beers to the field. Bluets stood strong as stars in the late afternoon. The lilies were tall as toddlers.

We sat in downy weeds, and I told her my name. Alma. What was hers?

"Bordelon," she said.

"That's a last name," I said. "What's your first name?"

"That *is* my first," she said.

She reached inside her bag, took out a pair of Jackie O sunglasses, and put them on in one elegant motion. She uncrossed her legs, sipped her beer, stretched out lazily in the grass. Sunglasses weren't needed in this light, but I took it she didn't care. Up close, the tips of her pink flip-flops were mud-caked and grungy. My own canary-yellow Keds weren't new, a rim of dirt staining their bottoms.

"Where'd you go to high school?" I said. "Not St. Gen High. I never saw you there."

"Didn't go to St. Gen," she said. "I'm from Opelousas. You went here?"

"Unfortunately," I said. "Grew up here."

Maps didn't show St. Genevieve. Most people who found us were lost. Watching the local news told you nothing—it started with weather, floods, and storm surges, then parish politics, then maybe a feel-good portion on pet adoption or soup kitchens or hymn-singing children pulling at your heart cords. Sometimes there was mention of a late-night house fire, or a rocketing eighteen-wheeler fatally colliding with a family-packed minivan of clean-living types. These were meant to remind us of the grim dooms of life.

"You like St. Gen?" said Bordelon.

"Sometimes I do," I said. I stood my beer between my knees. "I'm just kicking and living." That was something my mother would say, but I said it as though it were mine.

5

"I'm twenty-two," I said. "Graduated from St. Gen a few years ago."

"I'm nineteen," she said.

"You were doing what in Opelousas?"

"Living with my grandma," she said. "She raised me. She's dead." She said it plain and turned to look at me. "Don't say you're sorry."

"Wasn't going to," I said.

I wanted to tell her I understood, that I didn't want anybody telling me sorry for my mother too. I could have said all that, let the words spill between us, let the beer and starry bluets put me in the confessing mood, but instead I told her I'd been working remotely for a Louisiana lifestyle magazine out of Baton Rouge when the magazine went bankrupt and laid me off. I was on unemployment. Because, goddamn, everyone I knew who was my age was in a crushing job or out of a job and we'd have to get used to it. She had no equally angry response. Somehow I'd been talking for a full few minutes. For half a year I'd been alone, felt funny talking, didn't know how to control my voice, what to do with my hands. I felt, as my mother would say, a liable fool. A dolty-dolt. A dumb-dumb chickadee.

Then I said, "I've got internet at home, but it's faster here."

"Must be bad at your place, then," said Bordelon.

"It's better on the first floor," I reminded her.

"Mm-hmm," she said, tipping her head back, her hair glancing the grass.

"Bathrooms are better there too."

6

"You got porn you're looking at?" she said. She directed those Jackie Os right at me. "That why you want to be alone?"

"No porn," I said. "And just tomorrow I want to be alone."

"Bullshit," she said, but she smiled, then sipped her beer, sucked at the rim like it was a mouth. I thought I'd drunk a lot, but I was just through my beer's neck. I looked out at the cluster of flowering weeds leaning in the wind.

I could tell she'd only hear what she wanted, so I lied. I told her I wanted to be alone so I could turn up my music, crank the medieval speakers. I told her about articles I had open, innocent people who'd sat on the toilet and found a crazy-eyed snake. Bordelon claimed she knew someone who'd gone to the bathroom and seen a baby alligator swimming in the bowl.

"And I've seen a picture of an alligator under a parked car," said Bordelon.

"Read an article about that just yesterday," I said.

"They can come at any time."

"Well," I said, hopping up, snatching my beer. "Let's go take a look."

"A look?" She sat up, took off her Jackie Os, put her hand like a visor over her eyes.

"Bet there's something under my car right now," I said.

"Ha," she said, understanding. "Let's do it. Let's go."

My Honda, tomato red, bug-smeared, sat in the empty parking lot. The car had been my mother's. A blue faded hatchback stood near. I only peeked—the backseat was heaped with clothes and food wrappers and magazines.

"That yours?" I said to Bordelon.

"In all its glory," she said.

We were pretending to check for reptiles, just for shits, but I was watching her. I could get a good look at her now, backlit by the lowering sun. Her eyes with heat behind them, near-gold, a broad, confident forehead. Concentrate, I told myself. I was supposed to be looking for an alligator.

We wouldn't find any animals, we knew, and that wasn't the point. I crouched and looked under my car, and Bordelon crouched and looked too, her head and torso swinging into view.

"Damn it," I said. "Not even one."

"I was hoping," she said.

We swung our heads back up and stood. She was taller than me, not difficult, with me hardly over five feet, with very ordinary blue eyes, very ordinary brown hair, very ordinary small teeth. There was nothing humdrum, ho-hum about her. She was one of the most beautiful people I had ever seen.

I didn't know why I said this then, but I did: "What was your grandmother's name?"

I thought she'd tell me to leave the subject alone, yet without even taking a breath, she said, "Beatrice."

Beatrice. The name of someone no longer with us. I liked thinking of my own mother's name. *Naomi. Naomi. Naomi.* For now I could only hold the word in my head, never speak it aloud. It was like the syllables of a spell.

Naomi. The name had shock and thrum.

"Beatrice," I repeated.

I leaned on my car, and Bordelon looked down. Just like that, two tears fell from her eyes to the ground. I thought of the girl in the fairy tale whose tears turned to seeds, to sprouts, to flowers. We said nothing for a minute, just stood. Silence was as near to us as a third person. Something I'd started to know was this—grief was a string that held people together.

"I don't really need to be alone up there," I said. "It's not like I own the second floor."

"I get it," she said. She was still looking down, letting her eyes search the ground.

"I'm always alone," I said. "Maybe too much. I like the company." I half meant it.

She looked at me finally, her lids and lashes damp. I had no tissue.

"I won't watch what you're doing," she said. "I never do. Turn up your music, I don't care." She sniffled and smiled, rubbed snot from her nose with the back of her hand, her chipped blue fingernails. "Read about all the snake toilets you want."

I laughed, heard thunder. Raised my eyes to the lightning crazing the clouds. I was ready for rain to follow, but this time it didn't come. It was August. Any mild or mean weather could and would arrive.

I took out my phone, put on music. Something sulky and punk from the '90s. I had a six-pack litter of Abitas in my backseat. We sat on the trunk of my car and started in on those. It would be light for hours. I looked at her face every chance I could. Her smooth forehead, her eyes gone to clear gold in the light. Her hair was long and dark and frayed. I gave in. We both had another beer, and then another, as the night cooled and flickered and zoomed.

NOT EVEN NAMES

When my mother gave birth to me, she told me she felt lost to the stars. She thought she was in the sky. They had to strap her down to the bed. They had to feed her with a spoon.

She told the nurses not to worry—she had command of the starship. She was the first female captain, she said, she'd be in the history books.

My mother stayed in the hospital room, lost like that, postpartum psychosis. Nurses put me in a nursery crib, kept me, fed me, held me.

For the first month of my life I had no name. My father visited the hospital after five weeks. He cradled my body, pronounced me "Alma." Where Alma came from, he didn't say. What he made sure of was I had his last name too. Alma Lee Guidry. And then he was gone. He died shortly after. That's what my mother told me.

Maybe some of this was why I felt old and young. Born here, but not belonging. Old soul, fish out of water, little lamb, whatever you wanted to call me.

When my mother got well, six whole months into my life, we came home. The house in which my mother died.

I took care of her the best I could, but what did I know at twenty-one years old of tending to my dying mother? Ovarian cancer, the doctor had told her, and terminal. What she said was, in the end, she didn't want anybody but me—no doctor, no hospital, no fools, not anybody. If a doctor came near, she just knew she'd die faster, she said. They'd speed up cancer's work. *This is the way it should be*, she said. *Dying in this house, lost to its walls.*

She shrank before my eyes. Just small and bones, slight as a wren.

"Let me call someone," I'd say.

"Now who would that be?" she'd say.

"Anybody. Someone from church."

"Don't you dare," she said. "I've said good-bye to them all. I won't do that again."

For her weight, I'd fed her candy. SweeTarts, Baby Ruths, PayDays, Milky Ways, Laffy Taffy. *Hershey* was her very last word to me. She'd wanted a treat, a full-size almond chocolate bar. I unwrapped it, tore away the foil, placed it in her hand. She ate it little by little, in tiny mouthfuls, the way I'd once seen a duckling eat. My mother's teeth were rotting. In her last weeks, we didn't brush them, just swished water around her mouth. Candy collected on her canines and molars, made a white film on her tongue. Dying teeth didn't matter when you were dying. She asked for no fan in her room, the AC vent closed. It was hotter than hell or heaven.

She finished the bar, rolled over, went to sleep. When she woke in the evening, that was it. She wouldn't talk. For a whole week she said nothing. Only looked at me, her eyes going, or maybe already gone, to the clouds.

When she died, I made the phone call I didn't want to make. I felt I had to do it. Two Angels of the State arrived at the door. Dressed in white hazmat suits, N95 masks, and face shields, their faces blurred behind the plastic. They did not talk to me. They made gestures with their hands. *Where is the body?* I led them to my mother's room. They lifted her skeletal, imperfect body from her bed, placed her in a dark bag on a stretcher. I watched everything, everything, recording it in my mind. They zipped the bag over her feet, her velvet knees, her neck, her hair. They never looked at her face.

I'd reported her death. She'd never wanted me to. They were taking her for cremation. No burial, no grave, not what she'd wanted. This was federal law now, violations punishable.

They drove her away in a white, hearse-shaped Thermo King. For hours after, I walked the rooms of our house, restless and worn. I looked at all our furniture, all our objects, with new eyes, changed eyes. My body held the weight of such sadness, I felt my feet would step through the floor.

Even then, I could not cry.

Now, six months past, I slept in my mother's bed.

I'd kept her things, abandoning my old room, making my mother's room my own. I'd hung my graphite figure drawings on the walls, pushpinned dozens of them in haphazard rows. Women, mostly. Some in profile, some standing, slightly bent with hands on their knees, some with their arms straight at their sides. I'd drawn each and every one. Above my bed I'd hung a large figure I'd colored in with violet and red pencil. She was half bison, half woman, in profile and rampant, resembling a shape I'd seen in images on the internet of the Cave of Altamira.

The house had belonged to my grandparents. I had no money for upkeep, for the fraying carpets or crumbling grout. Our wallpaper had cracked from mildew and no-see-ums and must. The porch wilted from heat, our mailbox was syruped with rust. What little money I did have came from the state—minimum unemployment and sometimes some government account my mother had been paying into, working as a teacher's aide at the elementary school. When I was a kid, a great-uncle on my father's side sent checks. No notes, no cards, no return address, just a check, signed by and made out to the same last name as mine. *Guidry.* But a check like that hadn't come in years.

In early morning or in the late-night dark, I wrote poems. On nights I couldn't sleep—after I'd drugged myself by staring at the violet buds and thistles in the wallpaper, counting all the tears and dings I could find in the lamplight—I wrote. Hundreds of lines, written on scraps, dashed off or labored over, stashed away. Typed up on my ancient laptop that sat in a drawer in my mother's little oak desk. Maybe I'd hold on to them my whole life. Maybe they'd waste away when I did, whenever that would be.

What I knew about my own wasting away was I would not be buried in the ground. There was no such thing, anymore, as legal burial. The government had taken that away. Sea levels were rising at a faster rate. On the coasts, the ground eroded faster. Storm surges, whole walls of water during storms, were more frequent. Hurricanes lasted longer, grew in intensity. Flooding was more dire, happened quickly. We had to preserve arable, livable land. There had to be action, there had to be a gesture.

Scientists told us measurements, showed the changes happening the way they'd predicted, worse than that. Two years back, in 2040, the U.S. had begun Phase One. Our deceased were the first to surrender rights. Any act of burial was made illegal. The government gave a date—dying past it meant mandatory cremation. In Louisiana, and in every state, public cemeteries were reclaimed. Private cemeteries, even the smallest churchyards, were seized. Now all graveyards were government-owned—closed up, walled with brick or concrete, no visitors. Graves were left to grow over and be forgotten, shut away by weeds and moss and vines.

When our cemeteries were taken, we lost the ritual of loving our dead with the diamond of living too.

My mother had always wished her body to be buried, the place marked with a headstone, her name and years etched, a spot for ordinary flowers. Live long enough into the future, and some things become too much to want.

As far as I knew, after the Angels of the State took a body away, they went to a place of machines. Mechanical arms ushered bodies through the ovens. Ashes were poured into state-issued urns, factory-sealed, and stored away for always. We had no choice. We were all being ground to nothing. We could not even keep the ashes of our loved ones. They wanted to take from us our own mourning.

But something I'd been told, some small pearl that kept me going: there were exceptions. There were ways you could get the ashes back. For example, if the decedent was your only immediate kin. You had to wait six months. You had to pay a fee. You had to provide proof, fill out forms, stake your claim. This was what I'd been trying to do at the computer on the library's second floor. I needed information from the government website, applications to complete. For all that, I wanted to be alone.

My mother's urn, Identification Number BROUS440931, was sealed away. Locked in government-owned, climate-controlled storage in Baton Rouge, sitting among thousands of urns. Rows and rows of the dead, stored away, out of the sight of the living, and as quiet as the grave.

But there were no graves. There were not even names.

I woke to our crazed cats calling in the middle of the night. I still thought of them as ours, though now they were only mine. My mother had worried for animals. Storms had killed or scared away our stray cats, but others would come out of hiding. When she was alive, we'd feed all cats that pecked our scabbed driveway. Now I kept on. I went outside, part of me still dangling in dream world. I scooped the last of the Purina pellets onto paper plates in the carport while a dozen cats love-nipped my ankles or waited under my Honda or hung back in the feral weeds.

One long-haired tabby had a shaggy head like an owl's, a ridge of scars down her back. I called her Shane. Shane, I said, the world won't be cruel anymore. Tell me what they did to you. I'll kill them, those cowardly pieces of shit.

I took a night bath, a reliable comfort, and went back to sleep and dreamed of my mother. Woke to light with my thick hair still damp. I couldn't sleep. I was thinking of Bordelon from the night before, hearing her talk in my head. *Beatrice.*

I needed Purina and beer and hard cheddar for cheese toast, and today there'd be a squall line storm. That was what my phone told me. But I knew already—I knew the grainy scent before storms arrived, the rustle in the air, crumbling clouds, bruised sky, the flash of our cats crawling for cover.

I drove to the B&K as the dim sun rose behind clouds. I put on the Carpenters' "Rainy Days and Mondays," her alto crackling through my blown-out speakers. Ahead, steam rose from the road. Green swayed on either side— wildflowers, overgrown grasses, some stems capped with dandelion stars. I rolled down my window, smelled the rancid scent of overbloom. All the rain we got, all the growth and green—it was as though we were letting our flora live too much, too quickly. Ripe petals fell from flowers, lay on the ground like small skins.

But we were losing trees. We'd turned against the earth that now turned against us, and here we still were, ungrateful beings at heart.

Too many trees I had known in my life were dead or not themselves. Broken by one storm and then another.

In August, I wanted October. In October, the worst of the storm season would have passed, taking my August sadness with it. I imagined I would shrink the sadness to thorns, hide them deep in the earth with wet worms and roots. I would always leave the thorns. I would never dig them up.

I passed a penned-in huddle of Holsteins, the Giver of Life Apostolic Church, Heritage Gun, parked slantways next to B&K's roadside sign with magnetic block letters.

PIZZA PLATE LUNCHES
HOT TAMALES HUNTING
LICENSES PHONE CARDS

The store shelves were close to bare. Everyone hoarded supplies, fishing line, duct tape, gasoline, rosaries, bottled water, candles, batteries, tampons, toilet paper. I got some of my staples: Brown Sugar Pop-Tarts, Abita Turbodog, ramen, Debbie cakes. I almost forgot the Purina, but I circled back to the aisle, picked up a very old *Star* magazine I found at the back of a newspaper rack. I paid for everything with crumpled cash.

Outside, rain rushed the air. I heard stray calls of birds, like strident bells. Birds knew the storms better than we did. It was as if, when they called, they meant to warn us and one another. Some species of birds were dying off. The cattle egret, the tricolored heron, the spoonbill were all endangered. I wrote a poem about them once but got the names all wrong. My mother said humans didn't deserve animals and their sainted hearts.

I backed onto the road. Clots of rain pelted my windshield. The storm was still new, gathering her strength, but I'd show her what I could do. I sped up, let my tires skid and rock. I'd gotten good at rain driving. I was riled and wired. That was something storms did to me. I turned on the radio, set the dial to the weather. Take cover, they said. Shelter where you can. They were calling this one Miranda.

I needed to get home, get inside, make sure Shane stayed beneath the carport, so why did I drive the long way back, this time past Our Lady of Perpetual Help—my mother's church when she was alive, she'd be there early every Sunday, every holiday, large and small—the drive-through daiquiri shop, the library? Maybe my dolty-dolt heart or bird brain told me to.

When I passed the library parking lot, I knew why. Something in me, could be, had known—there was the blue hatchback, all by itself. Bordelon sat in the driver's seat, wearing her Jackie Os, waiting, while the storm swirled, clouds pluming, lowering, and ready to burst.

BAUCIS AND PHILEMON

Bordelon sat silent and still, staring ahead at the library, as if waiting for the storm to bear down. Without thinking, I revved and pulled into the lot, parked beside her. She turned and saw me, took off her Jackie Os, and started, as though she'd been startled out of a waking dream.

I left my engine running, ran to her car's passenger side in the biting rain. She leaned over and pulled the door handle to let me in.

"What are you doing?" she said.

I scrambled into her car, bringing rain from Miranda in with me.

"Close it!" Bordelon said.

I slammed the door shut, wrung out rain from the ends of my hair. Her backseat overflowed with clothes and flip-flops and loose papers and high heels and burger wrappers and Sprite cans. I saw a curling iron, an old hot-pink Caboodle, some framed photos stacked in the footwells.

I pointed to the Caboodle. "Where'd you get this?" I said.

"You even know what it is?" she said.

"My mother had one," I said. "Don't know where that thing is now."

"This was my mother's too," said Bordelon.

"Where's she?" I said.

"Don't know," she said. "Don't say you're sorry."

"Wasn't going to."

Her face turned into a child's face, a complete, drawn sadness. Her blue eye shadow had faded and powdered on her lids. I didn't want her to ask about my own mother, because that was the beginning of all the things I didn't want to say aloud. But she asked me nothing. She looked ahead to the storm, clouds graying the light, rain blurring the arched windows of the library.

"What are you doing here?" I said.

"Don't know."

I waited, but that was all she was going to tell me.

"You have somewhere to go?"

I was asking too much. She didn't even answer. She watched Miranda bluntly, a challenge. *Come on and get me.* Her eyes didn't blink. Seeing her face—it came to me that she needed me there for a few reasons I knew and others I didn't yet know. The world had orphaned us both.

"Come over," I said. I surprised even myself saying that. "Come to my place."

"I'm fine right here," she said. "Library opens soon."

"Not for hours," I said.

"Two hours," she said. "Two."

"By then Miranda will eat you up."

"Miranda?"

"I'll drive you to my place," I said. "Leave your car."

"Don't want to go anywhere. And I sure as hell don't want to leave my car."

"It'll be here when you get back."

"You don't want me with you," she said.

"Sure I do," I said. "And I've got beer."

That was what did it, turned her mind. She picked up her bag, and we ran outside, ducked into my car, the rain pawing and clawing our heads. She watched her hatchback through the window as we drove away, like it was a dear friend she was leaving. She kept her eyes on it until we were out of sight.

"It's not going anywhere," I said.

I thought we'd talk on the short way back to the house. Miranda was picking up speed, and I put on the Carpenters. But Bordelon reclined her seat and closed her eyes, hugged her purse to her chest. I wanted to rock and skid with the pooling rain in the road, show her my thrills and tricks. Instead I drove slow, creeping along in the storm, not wanting to stir or wake her. I smelled asters and wild carrot in the rain, felt heat on my arms and palms, itching my scalp and ears, heat touching my brain, my brain humming along, and me singing to myself, as if I talked to the world or the world talked to me, but my mother would tell me that's God.

Her eyes touched every object. She walked through every room, holding her purse to her chest. When she came to my bedroom, the room I slept in that had been my mother's, she said, "It smells wet."

"I know what you mean," I said. The damp smell had seeped in everywhere, all through the walls and carpets. So it was and would always be. A few times, on very dry afternoons, I'd tried to air the house, flinging open doors and windows, but the damp would come back the very next day. It was like another soul in the rooms.

I led Bordelon to the living room, fluffed a musty pillow on the sofa, right next to the glass curio cabinet of my mother's willowware dishes.

"Go ahead," I told her. "You can sit."

She held on to her purse, moved my mother's diamonded quilt to the other side of the sofa, smoothed down the skirt of her striped tank dress, and sat. Her eyes wandered and roamed the walls—family photographs of people long gone, ones my mother had put up so long ago I was sure the wall paint was a different color behind the frames. There was one of my mother, posing next to a Volkswagen parked in front of our house, years before I was born. The Volkswagen had belonged to a boyfriend. From a side table drawer I took out a collapsible camping cup and a miniature bottle of Wild Turkey. I poured a deep puddle of bourbon, gave the cup to Bordelon.

"I've got beer in the fridge," I said, "but I thought we'd start out right."

"Won't say no to that," she said.

I touched my bottle to her cup in cheers. Miranda's thunder shook the glass panes of the curio. Bordelon wasn't talking, just sitting with her paisley purse on her lap, sipping from the Turkeyed-up camping cup. I drank straight from the bottle, letting the liquid warm my throat, my ears, my toes.

Miranda gathered wind.

Miranda knocked at the roof.

Miranda shouted at the windows, wailed for our attention, but the Wild Turkey calmed me.

"God, I hope Shane's all right," I said. I'd always brought whatever cats I could find back inside for a storm, and always Shane, but this time I'd forgotten.

"Who's Shane?" said Bordelon.

"A cat who's been through a hell of a lot."

"Then she'll be just fine."

I told Bordelon a story Naomi used to tell me during a storm, a fairy tale of a couple, two lovers, a man and a woman who became trees. Two gods, disguised as mortals, had appeared at the couple's door. The couple welcomed the gods into their home for the night. The man and woman were poor, but they fed the disguised gods, gave them what they had. The woman gave them food, the man gave them wine.

Then there was a great flood. That was when the gods revealed themselves to be gods. They saved the couple from the flood. They protected them. Then the gods, thankful for the hospitality, said they would grant the couple one wish. This was what the couple asked: they wanted to die together, and peacefully. When it should happen that one of them would die, the other one wanted to die at the same moment. This wish was granted. When it came time for the woman to die, the man died alongside her. At their deaths, the lovers were transformed into intertwining trees. The end.

By then Bordelon had finished her Turkey. She'd been listening and sipping, utterly silent, her eyes on me.

"You make that up?" she said.

"Wish I did. I've got a book of Greek myths. Somebody gave it to me." That somebody was my mother, I didn't say. A gift when I turned seven.

"But I'm guessing you like stories," she said. She reached down and fiddled with a flip-flop, scritch-scratched at her toes.

"Sometimes I write poems," I said.

"I bet you could make something like that up," she said. "If you wanted."

"Don't think so."

"Bet you could, though," she said.

"How do you know?"

"I can just tell," said Bordelon. "I can tell about you."

She looked me up and down, all the way through. Some part inside me straightened and felt large, being told a nice thing like that. She was doing something to me, making me feel like *more* than I was, together with the Turkey and the myth and Miranda. I refilled Bordelon's cup.

"That story was a beautiful thing," she said, watching me pour. "We need more things like that."

"Who?"

"Everybody."

And then Bordelon did her own beautiful thing: she handed me her drink—*hold this a sec*—unzipped her purse, and took out a rosy Wet n Wild lip gloss. She twisted the top, pumped it twice, then ran the applicator languidly along her lips. I just sat and watched. I didn't know the reasons why it fascinated me, but it was an elegant sight.

"Wonder if the lights will go out," she said.

I felt Miranda breathe. The house seemed to warp and list and bow. We didn't talk, just sat and drank and listened. I thought about my mother hanging up photographs, collecting all those dishes for the curio, dishes that we never used, and me living in this house alone, hardly changing a thing. But I was letting the roof lose shingles, the kitchen linoleum pucker, the back stoop sprout weeds. I made myself think of something else. I imagined those mythical lovers as trees, hanging on, and then my head felt full, and awake, and brimming, the crown of my skull alive.

We'd fallen asleep. It must have been when Miranda subsided, the Wild Turkey luring us to dreams. I woke to Bordelon snoring. She was facedown, with the diamonded quilt over her shoulders, one arm dangling over the lip of the sofa, her hair spread like a veil.

It was dusk and calm. I went out the back door to see Miranda's damage. Upturned weeds, petals, and leaves covered the yard like a carpet that had just bloomed. The bench my grandfather built was loaded with scattered weeds and stems.

I went to the carport, calling for Shane and kissing my lips together. I ripped open the new bag of Purina, poured pellets on a paper plate to tempt her. I was all Shane had.

The nearest neighbors were half a mile away. I made a few more plates of Purina, scattered them in the driveway.

"Come back to me," I said aloud. Sometimes I wasn't afraid of talking to myself or speaking my wishes.

In the kitchen, I scrambled eggs—awful, runny eggs. Bordelon snored from the living room, snores ascending in tone, riding up a nasal scale. I brought her a plate and fork, set them beside her on the sofa.

"Breakfast," I said loudly.

Her eyes fluttered fully awake, her mouth twitched, and slowly she came back to this world.

"What time is it?" she said.

"Nighttime," I said. "The storm's passed."

"Is it coming back?" she said. "Is another one coming?"

"Not that I saw on my phone. You have a phone?"

Bordelon sat up, took an old cell from her purse, held it up so I could see.

"Barely works anymore. Old as shit."

"Lucky."

She eyed the liquid eggs, tucked her purse under her thigh, and picked up her plate. I let her eat for a minute. I wasn't hungry, with the inside of my head pealing from the bourbon.

"What do you have in there?" I said. I pointed to the purse. "Magic mushrooms?"

"Magic beans," she said with no laugh or smile. She licked yolk runoff from her fork tines.

"You should stay here tonight," I said. "I'll put you in my old room."

"My stuff's in my car."

"Can I ask you something?" I said. "You living in there?"

"Living in where?"

"Your car."

She put down her fork, pressed her lips together, played with an earring. It was a dingy silver drop, dangling from her lobe.

"Look, I don't care," I said. "I'm just asking."

"For now," she said. "I live there for now."

"Pegeen lets you?" I said.

"She just walks by me after she locks up. Doesn't say anything to me."

"You should stay here tonight," I said again.

She looked right at me. Maybe I'd said something right. "It'll be plum to sleep in a bed," she said.

"Plum?"

"It's what my grandmother said."

"Beatrice," I said. I wanted to show her I remembered.

"That's right."

I brought her to my old room. I put clean sheets on my four-poster bed, the one I'd slept in since I could remember. Bordelon watched me do it all. Even though now I slept in my mother's room, my old room wasn't much changed since I left. The mattress sagged, the overhead light flickered at night, and there were bugs the size of blueberries on the windowsill. I turned on my bedside lamp next to a photo of a twice-removed cousin I'd never met, standing in front of our house, long-legged and sixteen.

"No trophies," said Bordelon.

"What?"

"Everyone's got trophies," she said. "You don't have anything. No trophies, no ribbons, nothing."

"I wasn't like that," I said.

"Me, neither," she said.

I folded back the comforter like we were in a hotel. I brought her my plushest towel, a washcloth, even a new, wrapped-up bar of soap, and arranged it all on top of my antique bureau full of mismatched socks and old phys ed uniforms and stretched-out underwear. She was still holding on to her purse.

"You can put your magic beans up here, if you want," I said.

"Thanks."

She set her purse down on the floor, right next to the bed. I looked at her striped tank dress.

"You want something to sleep in?" I said.

"Don't need it," she said.

"I sleep in the next room," I said. "Bathroom's right there." I pointed. "Hot water takes a while, but it'll come."

She got right in the bed, turned off the lamp, pulled the covers to her chin. I closed the door without a sound. For the first time in months, someone was sleeping in my house, just on the other side of the wall. I was a little less alone. That night, as I fell asleep, I heard her sweet breathing, her breathy snores. Soon I dreamed of my mother, her hands pressed against my face, her palms resting on my cheeks. She was calm, saying something to me, too quietly. I asked her, if she would, to say it all again, whatever it was, whatever it was.

Books Like Stones

I woke with words I was trying to remember.

Through the wall I heard the mattress shift on the four-poster bed, and I reminded myself—Bordelon was here, snoring and sleeping and dreaming. She might dream of Beatrice the way I dreamed of Naomi, and that's what we'd been doing, side by side, in our separate rooms, alone together.

It was ten a.m. All I had on my mind was getting to the library. I didn't know if I should wake her. I knocked softly on the door, heard her answer, told her where I was going, did she want to come, and in just a few minutes she was ready to leave, her purse hanging at her hip. She was worried about her hatchback, her clothes, her whole life inside it.

Her car was still there when we pulled up to the library. Untouched and baking. She unlocked it, rooted around in the backseat. I stood by, the lookout. The parking lot was crowded. Pegeen's boxy tan Buick sat at the front, hard

31

water stains ringing the hood. A pack of Virginia Slims sat on the dash, and a rosary hung from the rearview. It was Saturday, maybe, easy to lose track of the days while I had no job. Bordelon emerged from her car wearing a stonewashed jean jacket, her hair in a ponytail.

People jammed the bank of first-floor computers, scrolling, clicking, pecking at the keyboards, looking into the depths of the screens, dead to the rest of the world. I could see them on their social feeds, something I'd decided to give up. When my mother died, her church friends wanted to make a memorial page on Facebook, write out memories of potlucks and crawfish boils. Some lady from the church called me up, told me my mother had said I liked to write poems. Would I compose a poem for the memorial page? That was the word she used on the phone. *Compose.* Someone—I didn't know them—posted a picture of my mother and me, and then everyone started piling on, thumbs-upping and hearting and sad-facing and smiley-face hearting. I couldn't stomach any of it, the cartoon hearts most of all. The memory of my mother became theirs. I wanted to remember my mother all on my own, as my own.

Pegeen waved to me from behind the long, looming desk. She was surrounded by towers of books that were about to collapse, toppling stacks of file folders and legal pads, an old-fashioned Rolodex. Her hair zigzagged in white waves down the sides of her face. I hadn't talked to Pegeen since I'd come back to the library, just given her a courteous hand up and hand down—*hello, see you later, see you, no time, see you!*—from a distance. All she'd want would be to talk about my mother. Bordelon stared ahead, focused on the slim archway to the stairwell, our portal—only mine, no, mostly mine, a little hers. Only ours.

Upstairs, it was as quiet as the moon, as a crowd of dead souls. Quiet, I imagined, as a graveyard might be. I'd been to a graveyard just once in my life. Now I knew that would be the only time. I was twelve and with my black-skirted mother. What I remembered—the long-stemmed bouquets in ribboned glass vases left at the bases of headstones of real stone, stony stone. A withering magnolia tree at the periphery, the magnolia blossoms faded to leathered bronze in the sun. And I remembered the names. Sarah, Elizah, Stanley, Annamae, Birdie.

HERE LIES BETH KAY

HERE LIES PHILLIPA

HERE LIES LEONA

Then older names, ones I'd never heard before. Hagerty. Aseneth. Elora. Headstones like small trees in rows, shadows striping the stone. Before my mother and I reached the graves of my grandparents, we came to a memorial, a two-foot-tall, stagelike platform with the marble figures of two children—Charlie and Ella—lying asleep, entwined on a little stone bed on the stage. Ella died in 1997 at three months old. Her brother Charlie died at seven months in 1994.

The graves of my grandparents, Arthur and Edith, were at the end of a path silvered with moss. Buried side by side, at their request. Plain, unadorned.

We knelt, my mother and I, tore away the grass that had grown over, uncovered my grandparents' names. We laid down the bunches of wildflowers we'd picked from our yard. My mother reached in her pocket, took out a peppermint wrapped in cellophane.

"Put it here," she said, pointing to the spot in front of my grandmother's stone. "An offering."

She placed the peppermint in my palm, let me be the one to set the round striped candy just below my grandmother's inscription. HERE LIES OUR SAINTED SOUL.

Since then, the graveyard had been seized and closed, walled up with brick, overgrown with weeds thick as fog. Edith and Arthur. Hagerty and Aseneth. Charlie and Ella.

On the second floor of the library, I had a thought that clung to my bones. Each book on the shelf was like a headstone, a grave. I walked by the stacks, scanned the names. Achebe. Dickens. Hurston. Ovid.

No one was at the row of our three computers. Bordelon and I were alone. The field through the picture window was blown through, tattered from the storm, but it was there, *here*, just feet away from us through the humid glass.

"You can sit here," said Bordelon.

She pointed to the window spot. I didn't argue and sat down. Even at this distance I could see the field's edges, lantana bold and clustering.

Bordelon said she was going down to the vending machines, that she was hungry, did I want anything? Nothing, I said. She said she'd be gone a little while.

"You don't have to," I said. "You can stay here."

She shrugged. "You want to be by yourself. I get it." And she took off.

I went straight to the Government Death Site. That was what I called it, but everything was under the Department of Health. On the pages about cremation, there were stock photos of smiling families with brilliant teeth, and also people alone, staring off rigidly, happily, into infinity. I located what forms I needed for Urn Claims. Here it was: Only next of kin. Only next of kin meant that I had no one else—I had always been an only child, and for most of my life, since the age of three, or younger, the law said, my mother had been my only living parent.

I typed it all in. Urn Identification Number BROUS440931. My name, address, Social Security number, employer (none), my birth date, my mother's death date, dozens of things. When I was done, there was an automatic email from donotreply: They'd get back to me within five business days. They'd let me know if they needed more information. This is an automated system. Do not reply to this message.

What I wanted to write back: *You never asked her name.*

Bordelon came back with packages of Nutter Butters, Chips Ahoy, Jolly Ranchers. I was watching a video of cats pawing and hissing at lazy dogs. That reminded me: I hadn't seen Shane that morning.

"Take your pick," said Bordelon. She laid out the cookie and candy feast beside my keyboard. I took a cherry Jolly Rancher, as hard and glistening as a jewel.

"I was talking to Pegeen," said Bordelon. "She's not bad. She's all right. She took me to the lounge and gave me a Sprite."

"If we stay late, she'll give you a Gin Hot Special."

"What's that?"

"Gin and Sprite in a Solo cup."

"She's a good talker," said Bordelon.

"Wait and see," I said. "She gets going and she'll talk both your ears off."

"She told me," Bordelon said, "about your mother."

I stopped at that, didn't say one word for a minute, just stared at a cat crowing at a dog on the screen.

"What'd she say?" I said.

"Nothing too much. That your mom died."

"Mm-hmm," I said. "Okay."

"I figured something," said Bordelon. "I saw the pictures. And you weren't saying anything."

"Didn't know how," I said.

"I get that."

I looked out the window to the field, to the trumpets of lantana. There was a place past that where I wanted to go.

"Want to get outside?" I said.

She nodded. Maybe she knew why I was asking her, that I was feeling I could tell her out there. She had a Beatrice, I had a Naomi, and all you could hope was that someone, somewhere, had the time to take pity on us all.

We stuffed our vending machine banquet into our purses, and I led us downstairs to a back door with signs— EMERGENCY EXIT ONLY, ALARMS WILL SOUND. I knew it was broken. Bordelon didn't flinch, didn't stop me from pushing open the door, and out we went into the field, the ground soggy from the storm, then through the field, past the field to a place I knew. I called it One Oak because that's what it was. A clearing with a frail, short live oak clinging to life. I hadn't seen it in months, and as we walked, I ached with not knowing if it was still there. But *there*, here, here it was, *Here Lies One Oak, here it lies alive*, its thin limbs hanging with silver curls of Spanish moss, sheathed in greener moss. My heart knocked on my chest with happiness.

We sat on the wet ground in the crown of the tree's shadow, surrounded by wild blossoms growing like small scepters. The treetop draped above like a bonnet.

We were quiet for a while, chewing and sucking on Nutter Butters, staring up into the tree. I was woozy from the heat. Ants crawled up my toes, bit my ankles. The leaves and ground sent shocks of earth through my feet, up my thighs. Sun in the leaves. Everything hushed and alive.

"What happened to your parents?" I asked her because I did not know how to talk about my own yet.

I looked over. She was lying down, her eyes closed, her purse beside her in the grass. I caught myself drawing her face inside my head. Her lips, her lashes. I was trying to get it right, the angles of her cheekbones jutting beneath her eyes. What I was really doing was trying to memorize her. If I looked, I could start to see real things.

Bordelon opened her eyes. "My father was a shit," she said plainly.

"Okay," I said.

"He came to visit me and Beatrice a few times. My mother was nowhere. Me and Beatrice didn't know where she was living. But my father would come and visit, always bring me a stuffed animal, no matter how old I was. He'd be fine the first day, buying me things, talking nice to us, but then he'd go back to being a shit." She looked over to me. "Don't say it. Don't tell me you're you-know-what."

"Wasn't going to," I said. But that time I was.

It was as though she were giving me something, confessing, laying out an offering I'd asked for so that I might give something in return. And I did. She'd slept in my house, she'd seen photographs, my mother's curio, snored in my old bed, and for all that, I felt I could tell her.

"It was ovarian cancer," I said. "She was fifty-three." Then I told her about my mother, those last days at home, my mother shrinking before my eyes in the bed I now slept in, my feeding her candy and the candy not doing a damn thing. I told her about Shane crying outside the window, about my mother not talking in the end, refusing or losing her will.

"We lived in that house my whole life," I said.

Then, for reasons I didn't know, I couldn't stop. Once the well in me was tapped, everything came loose. I told her about my mother's postpartum psychosis, her being lost to the stars. Then coming back down to the world. I told her the name of the hospital, how my father named me. I dropped each fact, each image, one by one, like petals, at Bordelon's feet.

What I did not say—my mother's name. *Naomi* was a name that felt like a chant. It was mine to hold in my head.

"Where's her urn?" said Bordelon. "My grandmother's urn is stored in Shreveport. That's what the certificate they sent back said."

"Baton Rouge," I said. "But I'm getting her back."

"You were working on that this morning," said Bordelon.

"How'd you know that?"

"I'm not an idiot," said Bordelon. "I'm a smart bitch." Then she did one of her beautiful things, which I was starting to realize were just ordinary things for anybody else: she toed off her flip-flops in the grass, lifted her arms, raised her eyes to the tree, tipped her head flowerlike to the sky.

"We're two smart bitches," I said.

I lay down too and closed my eyes, snow-angeled my arms and legs in the grass. After a while the sky shifted, a cloud swelled. I felt the sky's trance. I could hardly move. Dim cloudlight covered my face. With last night's Wild Turkey still in our guts, we both fell asleep in the shadow of the bonnet of the tree.

She drove her hatchback from the library to my house, parked beside my car in the carport. She stayed again that night, and the next. The first night, she took a long shower, changed into a T-shirt that said BILOXI in neon cursive and a pair of striped pajama bottoms. We talked about maybe going out for a drink but were too lazy to go. I told her there was a place on Government Street in Baton Rouge I'd gone to called Radio Bar.

"I miss bars," said Bordelon. She was smacking gum, drinking a Turbodog, painting her toenails a dusty rose color. She'd offered to do mine, but I said no, my feet were horrible, my heels like lizard skin.

"We've got one here," I said. "It's terrible and smells like toilet, but we've got one."

"Don't want to go, anyway," she said.

"I'll take you if you're curious."

"Not tonight," she said.

After her nails Bordelon moved on to trimming the dry ends of her hair with a pair of kid scissors she'd found in my room. I knotted my own sticky hair in a bun. She asked about any boyfriends I had while she made small snips. I told her there was no one now. I told her I probably wouldn't marry. I just didn't see myself doing it. Some people from my high school were already having children. I said the only person I could call an ex-boyfriend, Tristan, had been a musician, or liked to call himself a musician, but in fact he just watched videos of funny cats or played role-playing games on the computer. Bordelon said wouldn't it be something if that was all leading somewhere, and maybe he really was doing it now, having the rock-star life, bus-touring the country, sexing it up with groupies, trashing hotel rooms. But no, I said, he was living nearby, with his parents, in Sibley.

Bordelon said she'd had two boyfriends herself, one of them serious. She'd been with him for part of a year, back in Opelousas, but she didn't want to say any more about that.

"I miss going to this one place," she said. "A bar right by the water."

"Did you use a fake ID?" I said.

"No one cared," she said. "They let me in."

I could imagine her chatting up the bartender, getting her way. I was sure men stared at her all the time, kept their gaze going until she looked back, and I wondered how that felt, like having a camera on you always and you smack in the center of the lens. Even me—I caught myself memorizing her face again, drawing it inside my head. Planes of the face were hard to get right. The angles of her cheekbones, the slope of her jaw.

On the second night, we drank until the room buzzed, and I told her a strange thing.

"It happens when I'm almost dreaming," I said. "I imagine people's skeletons."

"Like bones?"

"Instead of imagining people, I think of their skeletons. Skeletons cooking meals, having sex, driving cars."

"Skeletons driving around?"

"Eating and waking up. Sometimes I imagine people I know. Some of them, I see their skeletons so clearly."

"What about mine?" she said.

"Yours is the clearest of them all."

That night she took her Abita into the bathroom and had a long bath. I heard her splashing in the water, crooning a springy pop song from last year. I went to bed early. I felt my body purr and zing. She turned the faucet on again, let the water run until the pipes rang in the walls like the minor chords of an organ.

MYRTLE

Never had my mother wanted to live so much as when she was dying. What she made me promise was that she wouldn't be cremated, that she would be buried with a gravestone in our own yard.

"If I can't be in a cemetery," she said, "the yard's the one place I want to be."

I told her I would do everything I could.

She said, "I mean it. Complete the circle."

Just as she died within it, she'd been born in our house. My grandmother was in labor on the living room floor, the midwife guiding, sliding, coaxing my mother's slick newborn body. For ten whole minutes, my mother did not let forth her first scream. When she finally opened her mouth, opened her eyes, the scream she let out would not stop.

Countless times while my mother was alive, I'd thought about her wish, about not reporting her death. About doing as she wanted, digging a hole in the backyard beside my grandfather's bench, finding a makeshift grave marker. I'd even dug a bit of earth in the yard before she died, hacking at the ground with a rusted spade. I made no progress. The earth would not give, and I made no hole or dent.

I'd heard on the news about people doing it, burying their loved ones in their own yards, getting caught—one way or another, reported by a neighbor when the rainwater washed a body up from its shallow plot. It was a federal offense, $50,000 in fines if you were caught, up to five years of jail time, and government seizure of the body.

Jail wasn't what scared me. In the end, I couldn't think of it—my mother's dead body intact, lying in the ground outside our house, so near to me. My mother's physical flesh and blood, her blood not moving. It was her physical body I was afraid of. Her corpse so near to me in the yard. I couldn't think of her body lying there in the ground, her hair, her toes disintegrating. And when I woke up—her body still there when I watched TV, ate supper. What if her body came up in a storm? I couldn't think of looking out the window, seeing her hand or foot emerging from the earth, not quite buried enough, coming back up through the ground.

With me, the only person in the world who knew she was there.

I never wanted to lose my mother's body, to surrender her. But I didn't know how to live with her buried in the yard or how to dig a grave for my own mother.

On the day she died, I couldn't even touch her. I'd woken in the chair next to her bed. Her eyes were closed, she was no longer breathing. All I could do was sit, watch for a while, struck dumb with grief, stay in her company.

I thought for just a minute—almost struck up the courage—of carrying her body to the yard wrapped in a sheet, her limbs draped over me. Folding her body up, sealing it in the ground, watching her face disappear. I couldn't do it. I made the phone call, reported my own mother's death. Me, the dolty-dolt, sorry-hearted Alma Lee.

On the morning of the fourth day Bordelon stayed with me, we drank beer, watched TV. Perky women on the shopping channel sold caftans made of fabrics in bright colors. Two easy payments of $19.99. We watched infomercials on synthetic diet pills and 7-in-1 insta-cookers. Then a game show with people rolling large dice for big money.

"Come on, big money!" I yelled.

"They have to pay taxes on that," Bordelon said when one of the women rolled right and won $26,000. The TV woman jumped up and down, cried right into the camera. I liked seeing other people cry on TV. I could feel my own tears coming, tears of simultaneous happiness and sadness for this woman who exclaimed she'd never had so much money in her life. I cried a lot when watching TV. Soaps and game shows and medical dramas and lawyer shows. Reruns of *Little House on the Prairie* and *The Waltons* on during the day, then *Matlock* and *Perry Mason*. Even I knew that what I was crying about was much more than fiction.

"How much are the taxes?" I said.

"At least a third," said Bordelon. "And she doesn't get it all at once. Bet they give it to her in tiny checks, little pieces at a time. You ever read about lottery winners?"

She had her dress hiked up in the heat. She held her beer between her knees.

"Well," I said, staring into the woman's eyes, "she's happy now. That's something." I never had near so much money in my life. At the moment, $362 was sitting in my bank account. Soon, but not soon enough, an unemployment check would come, or one from the state from the account my mother had set up. The checks were always different amounts, and I didn't know why. I applied to what few jobs there were in St. Gen, and I never heard one peep back.

We watched the woman crying into the camera, her eyes clear and lit with happiness.

"She'll find out later," said Bordelon. "She'll find out later how it really is."

Then the news started. A couple of neighborhoods in New Orleans were being shut down for good. In a few years, the land in those areas would be unlivable from too many floods. We were coming up on the thirty-seventh anniversary of Katrina. A newscaster was telling us all this from behind his desk in the studio, a large graphic of the Louisiana coastline projected beside his face.

Then a segment on protests. There was talk of the government officially making gatherings for public mourning illegal. Religious groups in our state and all over the country were protesting. They were some of the angriest. There were rallies being organized, people holding up posters. THE DEAD HAVE RIGHTS TOO and GOD IS WATCHING and JESUS WEPT. Whenever I watched protestors on the news, I felt my own sadness come alive. Whole families were there.

Children on the shoulders of their parents, holding signs. I thought of what we were doing to children.

As it was, each state stored the urns. What would they want with the ashes of our dead? To take away our memory. To take away our mourning.

Now they wanted to take funeral rites. Any public gatherings of mourning where three or more were gathered.

The pope prayed for America. The ACLU brought together their lawyers, started petitions, just as they'd done with mandated cremation. I'd signed a few of them the year before, but now I was inside the new normal, a slow sink to the bottom of an ocean. When a change first happened, no one could believe it, and then, impossibly, we did.

I took the remote, punched a button, turned the whole thing off. Bordelon tipped back her head and closed her eyes. She wasn't asleep, just still, holding her beer between her knees.

"Sometimes I think I'm already dead," she said.

"Sometimes me too," I said.

Sometimes I thought I could hear it all vanish. Even the edges of the earth.

The automated email from the Government Death Site came that afternoon. They wanted to see me at the parish office in Alexandria. It would be a thirty-minute interview. I needed to bring the applicant's (a) certified, state-issued long-form birth certificate, (b) license or state-issued ID, (c) original Social Security card, (d) utility bills (lights, water, gas) and three other identifiers from column E, such as a bank statement or lease. For the decedent I needed to bring (a) a certified, state-issued long-form birth certificate, (b) an original Social Security card, (c) $107 for application fee paid to the parish clerk, and (d) all of the following: any life insurance policy (she had none), marriage or divorce certificate (she had none), the last five years of tax returns, the last three years of bank statements, any of the decedent's canceled checks, any will or testament.

The final thing they requested was a personal item. The best thing, the email said, was to bring a photograph. If you had one—"if available to the applicant"—a print photograph. I clicked to the page that would allow me to make an appointment. I'd thought I'd wait weeks, but there was a slot for early the next morning. I checked the box, clicked Submit. Went to my email for the confirmation link. I confirmed.

I'd kept everything about my mother, every form and scrap of paper. Every piece of mail that came. All of it was folded and scrambled, some of it unopened, stored in a battered filing cabinet I kept in the closet. All that afternoon and evening I hid myself away—Bordelon watching afternoon talk shows and dozing beneath the diamonded quilt on the couch, snoring, waking herself up, then back to dozing—searching through each box, finding what I needed, willing myself not to look too hard at what I didn't. If I let myself look, if I let myself read everything, I'd be lost to it, drowning in the objects of my mother, unable to emerge or lift my eyes away.

* * *

On the road to Alexandria, we passed thick curtains of wild grasses and philodendron. I wrote a lot about flowers, even drew them in my late-night time alone. I knew so many by their names. Bordelon put her feet up on the dash, stared out the window. She wore her Jackie O sunglasses like a star.

She'd been the one to ask to come with me. The night before, she'd found me with the filing cabinet, surrounded by my mother's papers. She'd wanted to keep me company and take a drive, and also she didn't feel like being alone.

Hydrangeas rotted in front yards. Wild azaleas grew in packs. You could smell their rankness, the air brimming with sweet, candied stink. If my mother had a headstone, I would bring her azaleas. I'd pick each one—a quick snap of the stem from the ground—and fill my arms, my purse, my car to bursting. Yes, I could take these flowers' souls.

The Office of the Parish Clerk was a stand-alone building with a dented metal roof, a large frayed American flag out front, the rope dinging the flagpole in the wind. Two people sat in a waiting room the size of a high school classroom. A man and woman, both silver-haired, seated separate and silent, their hands in their laps. The front desk was vacant. I was carrying a large leather portfolio my mother had once given me for my drawings. In there were all the forms, birth and death certificates, policies and paperwork they'd asked for. I had also carefully placed a photo of my mother inside a manila envelope. It was my favorite photograph, the one that stayed tucked at the back of a drawer, only for my eyes. When I looked at it even for a moment, my body ached.

Bordelon and I sat in a corner, all to ourselves. A sign hung above our heads, MARRIAGE LICENSES, but we didn't see young couples there. One of the walls had a white line painted a few feet high, right on the brick. I'd seen those white lines before, meant to show the highest place the floodwater had risen to.

I looked to my right—the older woman sniffed, used a worn tissue to wipe a drop trembling from her nostril. There were Bibles, thin and thick, abridged and unabridged, on the scarred table. An industrial-size bottle of hand sanitizer with a grungy pump, a tabloid with a cover featuring a celebrity in trouble with the law. Bordelon picked up the magazine and began thumbing her way through, her bag between her knees, her sunglasses propped on her head like two bug eyes.

"These assholes," she said. She shook her head, looked right into the faces of a film star couple. I recognized them. The man had gotten in trouble for having an affair with the nanny.

A large man with a bald head came out from a hidden room in the back of the clerk's office and sighed and looked at a computer screen. Then he called out my mother's Urn Identification Number. I stood, picked up my leather portfolio. Bordelon looked up at me from her magazine and squeezed her eyes with a long blink. We'd agreed earlier— I'd go in alone.

The bald man called the Urn Number again, and I walked up. He opened a thigh-high swinging door, led me to a smaller desk, told me to sit. He sat behind it, in front of what looked like a new computer. A small placard was posted: URN CLAIMS.

"What's the State Death Number?" His hands were over the keyboard, ready for me to start talking. He wore a Saints T-shirt and bright blue braces. The Saints hadn't played in a few years. There was talk of moving the team to another state entirely.

"*Her* number," I said, "is BROUS440931."

"That's the Urn ID," he said. "What's the State Death Number?" He looked at the screen, not at me, his fingers ready to type.

I took the death certificate from my portfolio and searched for the number. He sighed and looked over.

"Give that to me," he said.

He scanned the quick response code, then asked me a series of questions to confirm the information on the screen. Full name? I told him. Address? Social Security number? Weight? Age? Cause of death? I gave my mother's full name, my grandparents' full names, as best I knew them.

He stuck out his hand. "Are you paying with cash or card?" he said. "No checks. There's a five-dollar fee for cards, credit or debit."

I put my poor little credit card in his palm. $112. He had a card reader on his desk and scanned my card through. He printed out a receipt and handed that to me. Screen, scan, swipe was all I or my mother was to him.

Then he asked me for every single piece of paperwork I had brought. I took each page from my portfolio, delicately handed them over, one by one by one, as though they were heirlooms. In some ways, that was what they were. He snatched them from me, began to scan them through a scanner on his desk. His braces flashed in the fluorescent light.

After ten minutes passed, I said, "When's the interview?"

"This is it," he said.

"What's it?"

"You're in it," he said. "We're doing it right now."

When the scans were done, he punched on the keyboard, looking from the scanned papers to the screen—up, down, up, down. The sound of him punching the keys—something about how slight the sound was against the mass of what we were doing—made me dizzy.

He handed me a piece of paper with instructions.

"Read it," he said.

I was to write out a formal letter, with specific guidelines for each paragraph, saying formally my relationship to the decedent, saying formally that I had no other family. I was to sign the letter with a closing statement. I was to have it notarized. I had three days.

"In three days," the man said, "you come back. You bring the letter, and you come back right here."

"How do I notarize?"

"Hold on," he said. He was looking right at me now. "Let me finish. If you are allowed to have the decedent's urn," he said, "you cannot bury it. You must keep it in your own dwelling. Ashes stay in the urn. Read the bottom." He leaned over, sharply tapped the paper with his pen. "See there? Read that there."

"*Ashes must be kept in the urn. They may not float in the sea. They may not rise in the air. You may not scatter. You may not bury.*"

"Okay," I said. "Y'all notarize the letter here?"

He turned back to his screen, smacked his mouth over his braces. "You go to a notary," he said.

"Where's that?"

"You find one yourself," he said. "They charge you."

"How much?" I said.

"Ask them, not me."

"Where do I find one?"

He didn't answer. Instead he took my stack of papers to a back room to make copies. When he came back, he had a can of Mountain Dew and my mother's papers. He put the copies he'd made into an orange file folder. He handed my originals back to me, moist from the can's condensation. I didn't know what I was doing or what got into me, but I had to say something. I said just what came into my head, letting the words leave my mouth before I could chase them back.

"Anyone else in this office think this is crazy?" I said.

He did not look at me. He put the folder in a metal stand on his desk that held other orange and blue file folders.

"We can't comment," he said.

I couldn't stop myself. "You can't comment," I said. "And we're all just doing it. Saying nothing like this. Going about our business. My God."

"It's my job," he said.

"I get that."

"And sure. God's involved too."

"You think this is something God wants?" I said. "You pretend to know it?"

He sat there, looked stiffly into my eyes. "We can't comment," he said.

He cracked open his can of Mountain Dew and went back to his work. That was all, he told me. We were done. Later, I remembered: He never asked for the picture of my mother.

Driving back to St. Genevieve, I rolled down the windows for the green smell of life, the rotting overbloom. I told Bordelon I didn't want any music on, didn't want to talk. She just stared outside, watched the wild roadside green scroll by.

My leather portfolio sat on the backseat. *The applicant. The deceased. The decedent. Here lies. Here lies paper.* What I wanted was her ashes, a simple thing to want. I could throw all the papers to the wind. None of these things was my mother.

"Hold on," Bordelon said. She took off her sunglasses and looked out the window, sat up in the seat. "Pull over."

"What?" I said. "Stray dog?"

"Pull over."

We were on a two-lane highway, a few other lonely cars and a truck tugging a camper behind us.

"Just tell me what's wrong," I said.

"Alma!"

"Right here?" I said.

"Pull over, pull over, pull over."

I skidded to the soft, grassy side of the road, stopped the car. The truck with the camper took off ahead of us. "Over there." She looked back behind us, pointed out the window. "A ways back now. You wouldn't pull over."

In the middle of a small field, a few hundred feet from us, was a tree. A bold crepe myrtle, stark against the weeds, blooming alive with fuchsia.

I turned off the engine. We got out of the car, and all we could do was stare at the myrtle. It was all on its own, not tall, and not *not* tall, but strong and rising, brimming with limbs and bright blossoms.

"I feel like we should do something," said Bordelon.

"Like what, exactly?" I said. But I knew what she meant.

"I don't know. Meditate, make a wish, throw a penny."

As if by instinct, by some magnetic pull, we walked side by side to the tree. We had no explanation, no reason it should be there, but there it was, *here, here*, like a rising flame, a flowering sword.

This Tree I Did Not
Know, the Candle That
Would Not Light

Somewhere in the atmosphere, there are sunlike stars. Stars that pull, all of it, everything. They burn at their centers, radiate from their cores, gather surrounding stars to them with each pulse. I read this in high school, at the time making a silent wish I might be a person like that, pulling everyone to me. Charisma. I didn't want to be a leader, just wanted people to talk to, but a sunlike star wasn't me, was never me.

The crepe myrtle in the field—that was our sunlike star. The sun itself was out, slanting through the leaves. Bordelon and I stared at the myrtle as we walked toward it, in the presence of something we did not understand.

We sat, stretched out our legs, leaned back on our arms, our palms on the grass. Bordelon's tank top belled in the wind. I looked up into the crown of branches, some curved like ribs, others gnarled like the head of a medusa. I'd taken this drive many times. I could drive it in my sleep, hung over, or in hell rain. The myrtle was new to me.

"I swear I've never seen it before," I said.

"Bet it was always here," said Bordelon. "Maybe you weren't looking."

"That's deep shit, philosopher," I said, and she laughed, her eyes stuck on the tree.

Stray ants crawled up my legs. I was sweating beneath my bra, under my breasts. I chose one clustering blossom on the myrtle and focused there. I stared into its center, the sunlight drenching the bloom. I imagined myself miniature. I nested within it. I imagined Bordelon curled and nesting in the blossom next to mine. We were just children, curled up that way.

Bordelon spoke in the silence. "You didn't tell me what they told you," she said. "I figured it wasn't good."

"I have to go back. Have to write a letter."

"Letter to who?"

"Some kind of formal letter. And it has to be notarized. In three days."

"They'll get you coming and going," she said, picking an ant from her big toe.

"Are you going to try to get Beatrice's ashes?" I asked her.

"She didn't want that," said Bordelon.

"I'm asking if *you* want it."

Bordelon crossed her legs, looked at the ground, started picking and tearing at the grass.

"I think she didn't mind disappearing. Or she just lived with it."

"You maybe still could," I said.

"She's not my only next of kin. There's probably my mother, somewhere."

"What'd you really call Beatrice?" I said. "Meemaw? Mawmaw?"

Southerners had many names for grandmothers, though if I'd known mine, my mother told me I would have called her a simple name: Grandmother.

"Just Beatrice," said Bordelon. "Her name."

We could hear, now and then, a car pass on the road, but beyond that, the world was quiet as stone. I wasn't kneeling, but I was. The crepe myrtle's flowers bowed in the wind. It wasn't Sunday, but it was.

"I could dump those papers right here," I said.

"You could."

"It's all horseshit. They didn't ask to see the picture. Just death certificates, birth certificates, all that."

"But they're your ticket to what you want."

"It's the only reason I keep any of it."

"I'll be getting a birth certificate soon," she said.

"You?" I said. "You're already birthed."

As soon as I'd said it, I knew what she was trying to tell me. Maybe part of me had been knowing without realizing. I could sense things growing. She stopped tearing at the grass then, looked back up into the tree.

"How far along?" I said.

"Don't know," she said. "Really don't know."

"*About* how far along?" I said. I turned to face her, but she wouldn't look at me. "Make a guess."

"If I had to guess," she said, "I guess a couple months."

"Whose?"

"Somebody I don't talk to anymore."

"But he knows?"

"He knows," she said.

"And?"

"He doesn't care."

"You think that?"

"I don't think it, I know it," she said. She turned back to me then, her eyes glinting in the light. "Beatrice and I lived in an apartment in Opelousas. When she died, I had to give it up. So I was just . . . staying with him. He worked a little. I was donating my plasma for money. They'd give me a card with cash on it."

"Where is he now?"

"He's an asshole, is what. He's a lunatic. Now I just call him Fuck. That's his name. Fuck. That's how I ended up here. Just driving out of Opelousas to get away from Fuck."

She had options, I wanted to tell her. But over the past few years abortion laws had changed. In Louisiana, abortion was illegal at six weeks.

"What are you going to do?" I said.

"Have him."

"And then?"

"Keep him."

"It's a him?"

"I don't know. I'm guessing."

"You don't have to keep it," I said. "Or him. You have a choice. Even the State of Louisiana says you've got choices."

"It's too late for that."

I knew what my mother would have wanted me to say. That Bordelon would need a place to be and rest, that I had to keep opening my door to her as Jesus would have done, and the Lord was watching. What I wanted to know was if my mother was watching.

"You can't go back to Opelousas with Fuck," I said.

"I know that," she said.

"You can't go back to an asshole. A lunatic."

"No shit."

"You have to stay with me."

She waited.

"You have to," I said.

"You sure it's all right?" she said.

I'd never heard her sound so afraid, or searching for something, an answer. Her eyes went straight to mine, locked themselves there.

"Of course it is," I said, and I meant it, and I hoped my mother was watching.

A cloud came over, spread in the sky like dark ink. It started to drizzle. The crepe myrtle bore witness to everything. This was what I loved most about trees—their silent acceptance of us, their comfort, like an offering.

It rained harder. We stood to leave. But I did something I can't explain—I went to the myrtle, looked up into the arcade of branches. Then I raised my hand and solemnly pressed my palm to its velvet bark. I didn't know why, but Bordelon came up beside me and did this too, pressed her fingers to the tree. I dug my thumb into the *V* of its crossroading trunks.

We walked to my car. Her pink flip-flops swished and shushed in the grass. The rain-licked windshield was fogged over. I turned on the engine, the wipers, the defroster. Bordelon ducked into the passenger side, arranged the seat belt over her denim shorts, her tiny lap. I looked at her stomach, too early for her to show. I signaled with my left blinker, seeing no one on the road, and moved forward. Slowly, slowly—I did not skid, did not let the car rock or bump or glide. Bordelon reclined her seat and closed her eyes, and as I drove through the rain, I felt a strange blur of fear, a dark singing through my body that began loud and low in my feet.

I didn't stall, I didn't wait. I would write the letter. I had no printer at home, and a laptop barely alive. More than that, I didn't trust myself to write such a letter. I knew who I could ask for help. Pegeen.

I brought Bordelon back to the house. She wanted to nap, lay out in the air-conditioning, watch reruns of *Press Your Luck* and *Family Feud*, paint her toenails an old color she'd found called Kiss Me Blue.

I didn't go into the house, but I did look for little lost Shane outside the carport in the rain. Shane wasn't anywhere. I poured out stale Purina on a plate as a lure.

"What are you doing?" said Bordelon.

"For Shane."

"Who?"

"The cat who's been through hell. Have you seen her?"

"Haven't seen any hell cats lately," she said.

I gave her the key, and she went inside, wet grass still clinging to her feet.

I drove off, headlong into the rain, turned on the radio, switched to the news. Representatives were preparing to vote to forbid public gatherings meant for mourning. No funerals, no wakes, no public shows of remembrance. Soon it would be against the law. Protests were held outside the Capitol. In Los Angeles, a government building was set on fire. The pope continued to pray for the people of America. I tried to imagine a god who understood the word *America*.

I did not mourn my mother with anyone, though funerals were permitted then. What I didn't know how to do was mourn her without *her*, without her body or her ashes. Did not know how to have a funeral for the deceased without any presence of the deceased. With the death certificate, the Parish Clerk's Office had mailed a state-issued candle—slim, the color of a pearl—and an enclosed slip of paper: *"You may wish to light this complimentary candle to mourn the decedent."*

But when I held a flame to it, the candle's wick would not light. I could not bring myself to throw it away. I laid it on its side in the bottom drawer of my bedside table, letting it roll and slide.

I arrived at the library just as it was closing, bye-bye, nighty-night, the books were going beddy-bye, Pegeen was doing her lilting singsong into the PA. The last patrons were leaving, the parking lot nearly empty. She set the phone back in the cradle behind the desk.

"Hey," I said.

"Hey, stranger," she said. "Was wondering when you'd say hello."

Her white waves came down the sides of her face like two ladders. She wore clear-rimmed glasses and chin-length silver earrings. A long, floating blouse, a silk scarf looped around her neck. She could look good, put together, but I always thought her lonely wildness showed. I could see through to her eyes, rimmed in pink from all-night drinking. She was about my mother's age, but my mother had dressed differently. My mother had gray hair that she'd pull back with a few swift turns, clip with a barrette the shape of a claw. When well, she wore plain cardigans and slacks to teach at the school. At home, it was jeans and holey plaid shirts.

"I've missed you," said Pegeen. "I didn't know where you'd been."

"Home," I said.

"I should have called. You've had more trouble than you can say grace over." She gave me the kind of look I despised, with great pity to the point of no hope. "Did you get my card?"

She'd sent a sympathy card, months ago, with a cartoon basket of kittens on the cover. Inside she'd written, *Naomi will be missed by all.* My mother would have liked it. My mother would have put the card up on the mantel, let it sit there for a year. But what was I going to do with a picture of a basket of kittens? And who would truly miss my mother besides me?

"I got it."

"Not that I have your cell number," she said. "But we've barely talked."

"I've been upstairs, mostly," I said.

"I figured you needed time. Everyone needs time. How've you been?"

"Okay," I said. "All right." I cut my eyes to hers. "I'm not in the mood to talk about her." She knew I meant my mother.

"I asked about you, my dear," she said.

Pegeen had gone to school with my mother, been in the same class at St. Gen High. They were friendly, not close. My mother's only enemy in life had been my father. Maybe Pegeen was glad to think of my mother now, happy that she had not been the one to lose just yet in the Good Lord's Cancer Lottery.

"Hanging in there?" she said.

I hated that expression, for no good reason other than the fact that people said it all the time.

"Yes, hanging on," I said. "In there."

"So, my dear," she said. "You need a Gin Hot."

She knew I wouldn't turn that down. Ten minutes, and we were sitting behind the desk, drinking Gin Hot Specials from Solo cups. Just for shits, she recited facts and trivia she'd picked up from the day. People called the library to ask about anything they wanted. Some people were so lonely you could feel it through the telephone, she said. She liked talking to lonely people, because lonely people listened to you, she said. Other people just loved to talk, and when you talked, they were only thinking of one thing—the next thing *they* were going to say. But lonely people—lonely people listened. The truth was, Pegeen loved to talk too.

"You know who makes the best beer?" she said. "Monks. Monks have got breweries. Found that out this morning."

"Monks, huh?" I said. "I bet because they're celibate."

"Monks don't fuck."

"Pegeen! You go to church."

"Only sometimes," she said. "And. *And*. Did you know there's a whole army made of terra-cotta?"

"Terra-cotta," I said. "Like clay?"

"Enormous army. It's all in a mausoleum. For the first Chinese emperor. E*nor*mous."

As far as I knew, she had nobody to talk to at the end of the day. Her husband, Innis, was dead. She had no children of her own, parents gone, no siblings.

"What else you got?" I said.

"Well," she said. "Shakespeare never left England."

"Damn," I said.

"Now, Shakespeare," said Pegeen. "Shakespeare fucked."

In minutes the Gin Hot was doing its work. I felt my ears heat up, my lips puff and zing. A vase of immense false violet flowers sat on the desk—stranger and falser under the fluorescent lights. Pegeen was feeling the drink's zing too, I could tell. I almost forgot what I was supposed to be doing there. Gin Hot Special zings made me forget things like that. We were getting high off doing what you weren't supposed to do in the library—drinking, talking loud enough to wake the dead. Pegeen lapped me on the second round. She threw her head back, took a loud, large gulp. She wiped her lips with the end of her scarf. I knew that kind of drinking, going faster and faster with each round just to get to the next.

"I have to write a letter," I told her.

"Which one? A, B, W, O?" she sang.

"I have to get the letter notarized."

"Put your hand right there." She pointed to the desk. "I'll notarize you right here."

"The letter," I said. "I have to get the letter notarized."

"Hey," she said. "I said give me your hand." She pointed to the desk again. "Put your hand right there."

I did as she said and put my hand *right there*, palm up in front of her. Then she took her large date stamp and pressed and rolled it into my hand.

"There, my dear," she said. "You are notarized."

I took my hand away, rubbed at the red ink on my palm.

"I'm serious," I said. "You want to help me write and print this thing up? Don't you help people with things like that?"

I told her about what I had to write, how I had to write it.

"Bureaucracy," she said. "Tyrants. Animals. Beasts."

I told her there was a certain way it had to be done. I had directions.

"Those fucking fuck-fuck fucking fuckers," she said. "You know they'll come for libraries next."

I told her I had three days for the letter.

"They're all becoming robots. It's all machines."

"I have no idea how to—" I said.

"The robots are winning," said Pegeen. "We're going to think and dream what they tell us to think and dream."

"I dream about my mother," I said.

"Keep it that way. Don't let the fuckers win."

Pegeen rolled her chair over to the computer, turned it on. The sound of the chime.

"You and me," she said. "Let's write this thing. Give them what they want. Pretend we're good little girls." She pulled the end of her scarf from around her neck, shed it like a long skin.

"Not *now*," I said. "You're like a spinning top."

"I'm spinning into orbit, my dear. I'm leaving the atmosphere." She rolled her chair back to me, put her face in mine, exhaled her spicy gin breath. "Take advantage now. This is when I start to float. When I reach my omega point."

"Omega point?" I said.

"Besides," she said, "tomorrow I'm not here. Tomorrow I've got the day off."

I dumped my whole purse on the desk. The crumpled instructions rolled out with a gush of loose Life Savers and pennies. I smoothed out the paper, Pegeen refilled her drink, and we got to work, stating my relationship to the decedent, stating my Social Security number, the decedent's Social Security number, my full name and birthplace, the decedent's full name and birthplace, and on and on and on, all leading up to a closing line I was to handwrite and sign.

I hereby declare that, to the best of my knowledge, under penalty of perjury of law, the decedent is my only next of kin.

Signed,

[Your signature]

Your full name

Date

For two tipsy hours I talked while she typed. Pegeen brought out a sleeve of Oreos, a box of expired Christmas Tree Cakes, a plastic barrel of Cheez Balls. We were like two high schoolers writing the late-night book report, though I was asking for no less than the ashes of my dead mother, the deceased, the decedent. I thought of the leather portfolio still on my car's backseat, the picture of my mother that was mine, only mine. Pegeen was firing off, talking and drinking, drinking and typing, reaching within herself some level of elation known only to her, bringing her to a plane higher than heaven or happiness.

"Oh," she told me. "And son of a gun, I know a notary."

"How much do they cost?"

She chicken scratched a name and address on a Post-it. "Her name's Josephine. Lives in St. Francisville. She doesn't have a cell phone. You just have to go. Get thee to a notary!"

Then the gin hit me and Pegeen in new and rebellious ways. We were screaming out, ginning up, cutting up. I took over the keyboard, typed at the bottom of the letter.

Hear ye, hear ye,

Here lies I, the undersigned, Alma Lee Guidry.
I hereby declare:
FUCK YOU YOU PIECE OF SHIT PARISH
CLERK
YOU TURD BAG OF HORSESHIT FUCKING
FUCKEROUS FUCKERS

"Fuck the fuckers!" exclaimed Pegeen. "Fuck the fuck-erous fuckers! Fuck the parish clerk, that acorn, that worm toad!" She took a drink. "I wish we could write that. For now, they've got to think we're good girls. We've got to fool them." She took another drink, stood up fast, and shouted. "That codfish shitbat coward, thy toadstool, tiny liver!"

"Shakespeare," I said.

"Nope," said Pegeen, sitting back down. "That's all me."

I drove home at dawn, the letter signed and sealed in my purse, the gin knocking against my head, pitching at my earlobes.

I was over the limit. It started to rain. I scanned the glossy roads for cop cars, cameras over haloed stoplights. Sometimes when I drank I thought about what felt here and not here. The rain—that was *here*. My mother had been here. Here, here lies. Any tree I saw, that was *here*. Cell phones felt *not here*. Forms and paperwork were *not here*. My body, what I felt in my body, was *here*.

The sounds of two words rang in my head. *Gin, ink.* Words made their own sense to me through sound. Rain gin-and-inked the windshield. Rain gin-and-inked the traffic light. When I got home, I'd write this down, if I remembered. That was the hard part, to remember.

I parked crookedways in the carport. I saw no Shane, but the Purina had been eaten. The front door was open. I needed my own bed. I had an alcohol fire going in my sore head, my brain lights about to cut out. In the living room, Bordelon was asleep on the couch, snoring in front of the TV, the warbling sounds of an old man. Her hair fanned around her, her feet up on the armrest. On TV, a celebrity was busy buying her dream home, a heated pool, an indoor basketball court. All that seemed as far away as the moon. But Bordelon, the baby inside Bordelon, were both *here, here, here*, as near as the wind, the gin, the rain.

Two Girls, a Lady,
a Ripe Fig Tree

The lines circled in my head when I woke. Emily Dickinson on pain and nerves and tombs. Sometimes, at night, my nerves were pinpoints of pain, screaming out to me, firing below my skin. Sadness opened new canals in my body.

Quiet down, I would say. Rest. Nerves, be still. Body, now rest.

I'd taken a poetry class at Avoyelles Community College the year before, taught by a woman just a little older than me. Frances Boone. Frances said that everything was dying anyway, it would all dissolve, all of us, all of everything, the whole world would fade to nothing in the end. That was why she liked to make things up, write lines in her head, then write those lines on paper, make those lines into poems. She wore long, button-up shirts, like smocks, her hair back in two braids.

I wanted to know Frances better, tried to ask her questions after class, simple things, how she started writing, teaching, but she said, "I don't discuss the personal stuff."

"Oh."

"That's for my poetry," she said. "Nothing against you."

I found Frances Boone online, a public Instagram account. She gave her own late-night poetry readings, but she read topless, with one arm over her chest, covering her plump, fleshy breasts. Her eyes locked on the camera, she recited her own lines, the trace of a nipple peeking from beneath her arm.

She had, she said, an OnlyFans account. I never visited this, though I wanted to.

I said nothing to real-life Frances about finding online Frances. I said nothing to my classmates, who I didn't talk to anyway. Her poetry readings were my own discovery. She used words like *sluicing, plashing, derecho, pudendum, nasturtium, ribboning*. Some of the words I had to look up. Her poems were about lovers, past and present, the weather, deer, wildflowers, penises, her mother named Anne, the president, the Supreme Court, areolas, ice caps, vaginas, the ACLU, glaciers, ADHD, her father named Leighton, the Atchafalaya River, the planet, the endangered pelican, the morning, the evening, the dusk, the moon.

Hungry, hung over, I made a greasy breakfast at noon, an awful breakfast, bacon and buttered bread. I woke Bordelon.

"Come eat," I said.

Mascara flecked the skin under her eyes. She wore makeup nearly every day. I could ask her to teach me some things if I had the courage.

We sat down at the little Formica kitchen table. I'd laid out jars of jam and honey. I gave her a white, chipped plate. She opened the blackberry jam and dipped her knife into the jar.

"What about going to a doctor?" I asked.

"Haven't been in a few years," said Bordelon. "No insurance."

"You've got to go now," I said. "There's a clinic here."

"Going's not going to change the facts."

"I'm not talking about changing facts," I said. "But they can tell you things. You have to stop drinking. You don't know what that's doing to the baby."

"They're going to poke at me, tell me what I already know. I'm pregnant. I can't pay for that."

"I can—a little," I said.

I could tell from the way she didn't answer that she wanted to change the subject.

"What happened last night?" she said.

I told her about writing the letter with Pegeen, the Gin Hot Specials. She tongued off the jam from her blackberry toast while I talked. I ate my own bacon fast, hoped it would soak up the gin still flowing in my blood.

"Fuckers everywhere," I said. "In that parish office they're real fuckers."

"Of course they are."

"And you don't want Beatrice's ashes back? Ever?"

"I don't know," she said. "Maybe I do."

"You don't *know*?"

"I can't do anything about it. I put it out of my mind. That's what it is. Nothing I can do." She put down her jamless bread. "I can't eat," she said.

"Aren't you supposed to be starving? And get sick in the morning? And crave ice cream and pickles?"

She shrugged.

I told her I was going to the notary in St. Francisville, and she said she wanted to come, get outside, maybe, she said, stop at Woodpecker Sno-Balls. She'd passed it before on a drive and had never been.

We got into the car. It wasn't raining. Clouds hung close, like great thrones. We went to Woodpecker first, a tiny painted shack, as pink as cotton candy, with lime shutters. A girl, maybe twelve or thirteen, sucked on a hard mint and took our orders. I got Rocket Blue Bubble Gum, Bordelon got Root Beer with Butterscotch. I handed the girl my poor little card. The girl swiped it on her phone. I signed on her screen with my finger. I started doing math in my head. The application fee, sno-ball money, and how much would the notary be? An unemployment check had come three weeks earlier. I'd heard nothing from the weekend receptionist job at a tire place I'd applied to last week.

We slurped and crunched our melty cones on a sticky wood bench by the stand, clutched our purses between our knees. It was Saturday afternoon, but no one was there.

"I wish we could have a sno-ball every damn day," Bordelon said. "That would be plum." *Plum* didn't sound natural from her, but I didn't say anything about that.

"That's what Beatrice would say," I said.

"Maybe the notary will want a sno-ball."

"Does the baby like it okay?" I asked. "I heard sugar makes them jump."

"I don't feel anything," she said. Her lip gloss was coming off on her sno-ball, a rougy pink staining the brown root beer.

"Nothing?"

"Maybe one jump," she said.

"That's something."

"Maybe a kick. Just one time."

She finished her sno-ball, unzipped her purse, and took out a plastic jar. She stuck in her fingers and fished out two gummies, stuck them in her mouth. I looked at the jar. Prenatal vitamins.

"Your magic beans?" I said.

"I found them cheap."

"We need to go to a doctor."

"Quit about the baby," she said. "We're in public."

We reached St. Francisville by late afternoon. My cell phone GPS took us to a shotgun house at the end of Deer-haven Lane. The sun cooked the roof, its paint shedding in long sheets below half a brick chimney—the top, I bet, taken off by a storm. Bordelon and I walked in our flip-flops through the front yard, the steamy grass kissing our ankles. A woman opened the front door before I could knock, leaving the screen door between us. She wore a stained, striped button-up with the sleeves rolled, a dirty cap with red letters: MCILHENNY TABASCO. Her gray hair came out on the sides like two wings.

She squinted through the closed screen. Said nothing at all, just squinted.

"I need something notarized," I said. "Are you Josephine?"

"I am."

"I've got a letter, needs to be notarized. Pegeen told me about you."

"Pegeen?"

"Pegeen at the St. Gen Library?" I said. "Sorry. I know it's Saturday."

"Don't matter the day," she said. She held open the screen for us. "Wipe your feet, please."

Bordelon and I swiped our flip-flops on the straw mat. The living room was a shock of glass and wood and porcelain dolls, all the dolls inside a large glass case. A clock ticked above the mantel. I'd never seen so many wondering doll eyes. Josephine led us to a 1950s green and yellow kitchen. Laid out on an old wood table were stacked piles of newspapers, brochures about local elections and gum disease. The fridge made noises from the inside.

Bordelon sat right down. "It's hotter than fires of hell," she said.

"Cost is seventeen even," said Josephine. She opened a cabinet, got two glasses down. Around her neck she wore a thin gold chain with a cross the size of a dime.

"It's a letter for ashes," I said. "'Only next of kin.'"

"For you?" said Josephine.

"For me."

Josephine stopped, looked at me suddenly, sweetly. It was the kind of look I might be afraid of, but her look was different. Her face did not have pity. The look was not hopeless, not looking at me from a distance. No, to me—her look was here, right here, living and sad and burning. I felt it calm me, open channels up and through my body.

"You poor child," she said. "You're too young for such a thing." She looked over to Bordelon. "Both of you, just children." She turned on the tap, started filling the glasses. "Special discount for young people. I'll make it eight dollars. I can't take cards or checks."

"I don't have cash," I said.

"Hold on," said Bordelon. "I've got it."

Josephine set the two glasses of water on the table. "Drink, drink," she said. "You've got to drink in this heat. Be right back," she said, and she was gone.

Above the sink, out the window, was a view of a vast yard. A few stone pots of fragile shrubs surrounded by something that looked like the remains of a garden, a metal pinwheel standing still with no breeze to blow it. An oxidized truck sat like a sleeping beast.

"Wonder what she grows," I said. "Looks like fruit out there."

"I'd eat that," said Bordelon.

"Thought you weren't hungry."

I turned back to Bordelon, sitting at the table. She was drinking her water, her feet up on the other chair. She rubbed one of her calves the way a runner would.

"Something hurt?"

"Can't explain it. Everything's different."

"You know you don't have to pay for anything," I said.

"I know I don't," she said. "I want to. You're helping me, I'm helping you. We're friends."

My heart did a skid and hop when she said that, like I'd waited and waited for her to say such a plain, beautiful thing.

Josephine came back in, holding a round stamp and a pen.

"Here we go," she said. "I just need the letter." I brought it out and signed with Josephine's pen.

Josephine stamped the signature and signed too. Bordelon pulled out a cracked red leather wallet from her purse, brought out a twenty. Josephine took out a change purse, gave Bordelon a ten and four singles.

"That's too much change," said Bordelon.

"Keep it," said Josephine. "The ashes," she said to me. "They're your mother's?"

"Yes."

She looked at the letter. "Naomi," she said. "Naomi in St. Genevieve." Then she closed her eyes, put her hand on the letter, bowed her head, and moved her lips. I looked at Bordelon, who shrugged.

"If they don't give her to you," said Josephine, raising her head, "I want to know."

"Why?" I said.

"Just do, is all. You come and tell me if they don't. But they will." Josephine folded the letter into three for me, ran her fingernails along the creases. "Where will you put the urn?"

"Haven't thought about it. The mantel, I guess."

"Well. Start thinking."

Josephine looked over to Bordelon, who was rubbing and squeezing her feet and toes. She was acting like she was desperate and days away from birth, but she'd already told me I couldn't understand the way her body felt.

"Let me give you some of my figs," said Josephine.

"We don't need any," I said.

"I've got too many. You'd be doing me a favor."

She must have heard us talking when she was in the other room, Bordelon saying she wanted something.

"I'll take one," said Bordelon. "I'll chew on one right now."

Josephine led us out a back door. I could see now that the green was all untamed, broken by the storms. In one of the stone pots, a small tree carried swollen fruit. Josephine touched its soil with her hands.

"This one comes inside on bad days," she said. "Here. Pick. As many figs as you want."

Bordelon snatched three at the stems. I picked one, eased the sphere off its branch gently. The fig prickled in my hand. I bit, feeling tang and tart, the fig's insides a red galaxy of seeds.

"What else are you growing?" I said.

"Simple things," said Josephine. "Tomatoes, turnips. Storms come and tear them all up. But planting is something I do for me. Calms me down."

In the light, Josephine's skin was like aged silk. A cleft chin. Old warps and dents along her forehead and cheekbones. A wide scar crosshatched her upper lip, traveled lengthwise down to her chin.

"You want to help?" Josephine said to me.

81

"With what?" I said.

"I was going to plant today."

"I wouldn't know what I was doing."

"Doesn't matter. The way I do it, you can't mess things up," she said.

"Bet I could."

"Well," she said, "I leave it to you. You can help with what you want."

I thought of my mother, who'd always talked about planting roses and never had. I'd never offered to help her.

"All right," I said. "I can try."

Josephine brought out a lopsided lawn chair and put it in the shade. Bordelon sat down happily. Josephine took a pair of crinkled garden gloves from her pocket, put them on over her sun-worn hands.

"I lost my extra pair," she said. "But you've got young hands."

She took out a plastic baggie of fingernail-size seeds. She held them up to my eyes, but I was looking at her—her own eyes were blue as the eggs of a starling. Josephine took out seven seeds, opened my palm. They gleamed like copper in my hand.

"Cukes," she said.

I was new to most things in a garden. Josephine knelt before the tattered plot and cleared a few dying sprouts, broken stems. Wild bunches of flowers with pulpy orange centers grew at the edge. I knelt beside her, did just as she did. The dirt grimed my fingernails. Mosquitoes came at me from all sides. Wind chimes made tinny music behind me. I watched the metal pinwheel make lazy turns. One, two, three.

"I leave some weeds in there," she said. "Don't pick them all out. They're part of it."

Josephine poured new soil from a bag onto the earth and bore into the mounds with her knuckles. She filled the watering can from the spigot at the side of the house. We worked with the dark coming in.

We barely spoke. It was as if the garden did our speaking.

Louisiana made its rolling summer sounds, its choral chirrups of frogs. The pinwheel spun again, again. Ten. Eleven. Twelve. The air softened. The night greened. I was drunk without drinking, waltzing in my brain to another buzzy place. I let my brain carry me there. I felt bits of wild weeds stick to my fingertips, touching what grew in the earth.

I knew then that I wanted my mother to rest in green.

I would bury her in the earth, in our own yard, just as she'd asked. I could not think of burying her body, her flesh, in our yard. Her eyes, her lips, her neck. But ashes were something else. I could dig very deep and lay the urn to rest. I could lay a stone to mark the place.

We'd stayed so late the slow moon was up. Stars and stars. I stood before the garden and thought I was singing a song in my head that contained no words. Josephine washed her hands at the spigot. Bordelon stared up at the sky, her flip-flops beside her, her bare feet in the grass. Saturn was up. Her feet damp in the dew.

Monday

Bordelon and I were home past midnight on Saturday, slept most of Sunday, but Sunday night I did not sleep, reading and rereading the letter, brushing my fingers over Josephine's stamp, folding it and sealing it, waiting to leave at five a.m. to make the clerk's office at eight, which I did, dutifully, the first one in, leaving the letter with a tall woman at the desk. She was round-faced, her cheeks and chin stippled and flushed, as red as a prickled beet. I looked back when I got to the door. She placed the letter in a random stack—anonymous, out of her mind and out of the way—then looked back to her phone.

In the parking lot, a stray dog followed me to my car, the color of an Angus cow. I put my hand to her tan muzzle, gave her my fingers to lick. I had no food in the car. She stared into me the way dogs do. Her nipples hung down like she'd been nursing a whole litter. Her ribs stood out like teeth on a comb.

For a moment I imagined taking the dog with me, letting her bound into my backseat, her tail thumping against the window, buying her treats on the way home. My mother had never let me have a dog, on account of the cats, worried they'd wander away. If I brought the dog home, Shane might never show up.

You could still bury the remains of animals. Animals were the one exception to mandated cremation. No one had taken away that right. Pets could be buried on private land, in a backyard or field. You could mourn them the way you liked. You could have a headstone for your pet, build a tomb in your yard. You could bury your hamster, flush the corpse of a fish down the toilet, let your cat rest in peace. In death, it was better to be animal than human.

As a kid, I'd won a goldfish at a fair, tossing a ping-pong ball into a bowl. My mother and I brought her home in a Ziploc of water, named her Goldie Hawn, my mother's idea. We bought a tank, a bucket of mushed-up fish food. Goldie was a quick swimmer, darting behind the glass. She stayed alive for two weeks. When we found her faceup in the water, my mother clucked her tongue, said Goldie just had to get going, move on fast to the next world. In the yard we dug a hole with our hands, wrapped Goldie in newspaper, laid her to rest. My mother said a prayer, a terrific goldfish prayer, marked the spot with three stones. I'd stayed there all day at the spot, not crying, but keeping watch, keeping Goldie's soul company.

For my mother, I'd cried only once, just once, and even then, I was alone in my room, three days before she died. I kept waiting and waiting for more, for the tears to arrive.

*   *   *

I told Bordelon if I didn't take her to the doctor I wouldn't forgive myself. I told her I would pay. I told her I wouldn't let them hurt her, and if anyone tried anything at all, I'd stomp on their feet and bite their arms and claw their eyes.

"You'd do all that for me?" she said.

"If they hurt you."

But I knew she meant my driving her there, paying for it all.

I'd been to St. Charles Urgent Care before. They were cheap, kept Community Coffee and Doritos in the waiting room, gave out free pens and magnets. On the way to Alexandria, I gassed up the car. Bordelon said she was going inside the gas station to use the bathroom. She wore a tank I'd never seen on her, the kind that tied around the neck, and denim shorts with stray strings swaying. No baby poking through yet. A guy at the next gas pump had his eyes on her, every step she took. I stared at him while I pumped, wishing his eyes away. I'd claw his eyes out too—or anyone's, if need be. *Here lies you.*

Minutes later she came out with a Cherry Slurpee and a pack of Debbie cakes. On the way, Bordelon ate all but the last Debbie cake, not talking, all nerves and hunger and teeth.

I parked in the clinic parking lot, took a breath. I'd never done a thing like this before.

"Quit making me nervous," she said.

We walked into a half-full waiting room where there was a little window with sliding glass and a woman in scrubs behind that. Bordelon signed her name on a clip-board with a pen attached to a string. The woman in scrubs handed her another clipboard of forms. Bordelon and I sat side by side, across from an older woman—her hair newly curled, her hand to her heart. Bordelon started writing, in the neat, square block writing that reminded me of the popular girls at my high school. Did she put hearts above her *i*'s? My own handwriting was barely legible to anyone but me. I looked at the top of the first form and realized I didn't even know her last name until then. Bordelon Goss. I looked for her birthday. March 13. And just as she'd told me—nineteen years old.

"Don't watch me," she said. "Makes me nervous."

HGTV played loud on a mounted TV. A couple was buying a starter home in the desert. HGTV in waiting rooms was meant to distract us all from sickness and death, and it never worked on me.

"I don't know all this shit," said Bordelon, staring at the clipboard.

"Like what?"

"Cancer on father's side? Probably."

"Do your best," I said. "They don't expect you to know it all."

"I bet some people *do* know everything," she said. "They can fill all this shit out about their parents just like that."

"Normal people," I said.

"I have to write what I'm coming in for."

"Put it down."

"The p-word," she said.

She brought the forms to the front, handed the clip-board to the woman behind the desk. She pumped out two globs of hand sanitizer, rubbed her hands together, and took a handful of St. Charles Urgent Care pens from a cup and put them in her purse.

She came back, sat down, and leaned over the arm-rest—her face half awake, her arms crossed on her chest—watching the woman with the hand over her heart, no shame in staring. The woman's thick-lidded eyes were to the floor.

They called Bordelon in. Without asking, and without her telling me, I stood and went with her. A nurse led us into an exam room, told us to wait there, then left. We were alone. Bordelon sat on the table with the strip of white paper, clicking the heels of her grungy flip-flops together.

"I'm feeling sick," she said. She rolled her bottom lip under her front teeth.

"Vomit sick?"

"I can't explain it to you," she said. "Everything feels different."

A knock. I sat in the chair opposite Bordelon. A female nurse wearing scrubs with a lollipop print came in. She said her name was Mary Anne. She checked Bordelon's pulse, her blood pressure, her temperature. Then she handed Bordelon the kind of tiny plastic cup you'd get at a kid's party or from a watercooler. There was no lid for the cup.

"Urinate in here and put the cup with this form in the window," Mary Anne said to Bordelon. "Directions are inside the bathroom."

"I need a pregnancy test," said Bordelon.

"That's what we're checking for, honey."

Bordelon looked at me, left with the cup, and I waited in the exam room. Mary Anne typed notes into a computer and then, without a word to me, walked out.

I sat alone with the wall posters about diabetes, stroke, allergies, chlamydia. Part of me started to think I was sick, I might have these things, these silent diseases lying in wait. Whenever I watched pharmaceutical commercials, I always wondered if I had the illness that needed curing.

In a minute Bordelon walked back in and said, "Well. They've got their cup. I peed everything out like a water gun."

She got up on the exam table, leaned over and put her face in her hands, and just sat.

"I decided," I told her. "When I get Naomi's urn, I'm going to bury it."

Bordelon brought her head up. "Why?"

"She wanted that. Burial."

"Well, where then?"

"Don't know yet," I said. I didn't tell her I was thinking of the yard.

"How are you going to do that?"

"I'm a criminal," I said. "I've got it in me."

"You do?"

"Sure, I do."

"Show me."

"Let's take all the cotton balls!" I said.

I wanted to change the subject because I didn't know if in fact I did have it in me. I went to the plastic jars of wrapped syringes and condoms and swabs, opened up a jar, and I took, and I took, cramming cotton swabs down in my purse.

"What are you doing?" she said.

"Playing bandit," I said. "I'm a clinic bandit."

I took tongue dispensers, paper towels, Handi Wipes. I pulled out yellow rubber gloves from a tall box.

"I'm rich, I'm rich, I'm rich!" I said. I took Bordelon's bag and started filling it with the gloves.

"You're crazy," she said, but then she smiled, and that was all I wanted.

Mary Anne knocked, sat down at the computer, looked into the screen. Yes, Mary Anne said, reading from the screen, just like that, not looking at us, Bordelon was pregnant. No, she couldn't say how far along. Bordelon would need an ultrasound.

"Have you been counting the days since your period?" said Mary Anne.

Last one was months ago, Bordelon said, but she'd never been regular anyway.

"Did you take an at-home test?" said Mary Anne.

Bordelon said she had, but the line had been so faint it almost wasn't there, and she'd been too scared to take another one.

Here was a piece of paper—Mary Anne found the file folder she needed in a drawer, took out a flyer—telling us where to go in Marksville. Here was another piece of paper telling her good foods to eat. Here was another piece of paper telling her foods not to eat. Here was a piece of paper explaining what happens at each month.

"Also, this," she said. She held out a brochure with the image of a blond woman holding her child. "These people are going to come see you at the hospital when you have the baby. They're going to ask for your placenta."

"What people?" I said.

"They use it for something," said Mary Anne. "For research, I think."

"Research on what?" I said. "What do they do to it?"

"Medical studies," she said. "And tissue donation."

"Do they pay?" I said.

"Donation," said Mary Anne. "It's optional placenta donation."

Mary Anne stacked up all the papers, held them out to Bordelon, with Bordelon numbly staring at her with the most forlorn, drooping look.

"I'll take all that," I said.

I airplaned the pages and put them in my purse on top of the stolen cotton balls and Handi Wipes.

Bordelon wasn't talking. On our way out, I stopped at the front desk. The visit plus the test came to $129. I paid with my poor little card, doing pitiful addition in my head, rolling around the numbers.

Of course, it was raining. Bordelon didn't say a word, just looked out the fogged window. She took her Jackie Os from her bag but didn't put them on, propped them on top of her head. On the highway, I let the tires spit and skid on the road. Perfume from waterlogged grass and wildflowers came through the vents. The sun was gone behind cloud cover. Droplets careened off the windshield.

"No surprises," I said.

After a while she said, "I know."

"Nothing you didn't already know."

That was when she wept. That was when she let out a kind of cry I'd never heard, not from myself or anyone I ever knew. Something almost not human, beyond human. I said nothing, just kept my eyes on the slick road and drove. The crying sounded like something for which she needed to feel alone. She tried to talk again, but I couldn't understand her. She was crying the words out, choking on her breath. I kept driving, wondering what it felt like to weep long and true like that.

CULLEN

We drove back to the house, the rain so bold at the window I thought it'd shoot sparks. I figured she'd want to lie on the couch, turn on reruns of *Love Connection*, eat buttered toast, but instead she went right to the bathroom, turned on the tap of the sink for a while. I heard her crying more through the sound of the water. When she came out, she had little puffs of tissue still stuck to her cheeks.

"That bar that smells like toilet," she said. "What's it like?"

"You can't drink," I said. "I won't let you."

"I'm not," she said. "I'll get a ginger ale."

"Then what are we going for? Stare at the wall? We can drink ginger ale here."

"We'll talk," she said. "We've got each other to talk to."

"We can talk here. I've got orange juice. I've got Dr. Pepper."

"Alma, I need to forget things, you get it? Hear a little bad music."

"No live music at the Jansen," I said.

"The only thing I don't want to think about right now," she said, "is my own life. If you don't get it, you don't get it."

"No," I said. "I get it."

Bordelon went out and got her Caboodle from her hatchback. We went to the bathroom. We shaded our eyelids blue. Bordelon had a metal lash curler, told me to get the hair dryer, said she knew a trick. She plugged in the dryer, blasted heat on the curler. Then she put the curler against her lid and clamped down. When she gave the curler to me to try, I almost scorched my eyeball. I watched her paint liquid black lines on her lids, drawing them out past the corners of her eyes. She looked like a beautiful bird.

"Wonder if the baby can hear things," I said.

"Like what?"

"Like the hair dryer. The TV."

"With what ears?" she said. "You think it's got ears already?"

I sat on the toilet while Bordelon brushed my hair, unraveling week-old tangles. I'd almost never felt anyone's touch since my mother died. Feeling Bordelon's hand at the top of my scalp, balancing my head, made me shiver through my chest and my stomach, made a light blink on and off in my brain.

Side by side, we perched on the tub's edge and shaved our legs, water running as hot as it would go. We painted our toes a dusky color called Suddenly Rose. I changed into a dress that I'd bought in New Orleans years ago, with straps that tied at my shoulders and a tiered skirt. I felt clean and not pretty, because I never felt that, but I was decent, at least. Bordelon put on a yellow, crisscross-backed sundress, a gold bracelet that clung to her wrist. She was starting to cheer up, or acting so, spreading juicy lip gloss with an applicator on her puckered lips. Then she took the applicator and dabbed some on me, put a tissue between my lips, told me to blot. She looked at herself in the mirror, turned to the side, sucked in her cheeks. I saw some new part of her, or a part new to me, coming alive.

Her pink flip-flops were crusty and holed and mud-stained. I brought out a pair of my own sandals. They were made of black leather, rhinestones lining the straps.

"You like them?" I said.

"Love them," she said.

"They're yours."

"What? No, you wear them."

"They'll look better on you," I said.

When I looked closer, I saw that the leather was scuffed and frayed.

"Leather's fake," I admitted.

"No one'll know."

She slipped them on. I wished we both had a pair. They'd never looked as good on me, but we could have matched. We walked out to the car, with her smiling, her purse hitting her hip and her hips swinging back and forth. I wondered what she was thinking, if she might surprise herself by crying again. The skirt of her dress belled at her knees.

*   *   *

Gil Rue had called his bar the Jansen after his ex-wife's maiden name. He'd wanted a boat, but he had no boat, and the bar got the boat's name. The place was as dark as a cave, more cavelike still with animal heads on the wall, like a Neolithic pantheon. It was a stand-alone rectangular building with an orange shingle roof. It had been a general store, or pretended to be a general store. Gil Rue's family years back sold illegal corn whiskey, rotgut.

It was four p.m. and Gil Rue wasn't there. Instead, a young guy in an LSU cap was behind the bar, staring at *Jeopardy* on the mounted TV, calling out an answer.

"Who is Pistol Pete?"

Other than him, the bar was empty. Bordelon and I sat at a high-top table in a corner, made the bartender come over to us.

"We've got happy hour specials," he said.

"Where's Gil?" I asked him.

"Retiring."

"He never told me."

"It's new news," he said. "Don't get used to me, I'm temporary. Summer job. I'm Gil's nephew."

"He never mentioned you," I said. But it wasn't true. Gil had. I knew at least that his name was Cullen.

I asked for an old fashioned, hoped for a tiny red straw to sip from. Bordelon sat on a stool and put her paisley purse up on the table.

"What are you drinking?" he asked her.

"Jack and pop," she said.

"Just the pop," I said. "No Jack."

Cullen took off his cap, scratched his head with the heel of his hand. He was about our age, from what I could tell, a cluster of birthmarks coming down his forehead, right down to the bottom of his left cheek. They looked like a string of islands.

"We call that Coke around here," he said. "Where are you from?"

"I just like the sound of Jack and pop," Bordelon told him.

"Sounds like a nursery rhyme," I said.

He looked at Bordelon, looked all over, at her face, her chest, her feet. "Those are nice shoes," he said. "Saw them when you walked in."

"They're borrowed," said Bordelon, her eyes not on him, but on me.

"Will you put a little straw in my drink?" I said. "I like the little straws."

He gave me a salute, took up the remote, put a rerun of a Saints game on the TV. The 2010 Super Bowl against the Colts. The Saints didn't play anymore, and neither did LSU, but people still watched old games, nostalgic for their touchdowns and mascots and marching bands. Cullen fixed our drinks, put them on a tray, brought them right to us. They looked fragrant and crisp, but mine had no straw.

"Smells like crud in here," said Bordelon.

"Told you," I said.

Bordelon and I touched our glasses, rim to rim, looked each other in the eye. I tried to think of something clever.

99

She had to be sober, but I could help her forget some things for a while. I knew what wanting to forget felt like.

"In Sweden they say *in i dimman,*" I said. "Into the fog."

"Into the fog," she repeated. She smiled and smacked her lips. "Say it again?"

"*In i dimman.*"

"How the hell do you know that?" she said.

"Ex-boyfriend," I said. "Tristan."

"The one who could have been a rock star?"

"He's probably playing guitar in his parents' basement as we speak," I said.

I was making fun of Tristan, but the truth was, I'd been a pinch in love. In high school, Tristan had his driver's license before anyone. His muffler rumbled when he drove to the school parking lot in his junk Camaro. His hand had been badly burned. He said it was from trying to make a bomb at a boarding school in Virginia when he was twelve, and I half believed it. He gave me a book of poems by Kenneth Patchen. One of the last times I saw him was the first time we had sex. We'd ended up kissing on the floor of his parents' kitchen, with the lights out, his parents gone out for the night, their terrier sniffing at the floor around us. The house was outside of St. Gen, in a gated neighborhood. Tristan's parents had money, and he hated this fact.

We found our way, rubbing and jerking each other's bodies with our hands, our mouths, our teeth, his penis already wet. I ran my hand along its ridge. He got himself inside me, angling and mashing his way, no condom, no anything, not looking at me, looking at the floor with each thrust. My panties were still on, stretched at my knees. I stared at the ceiling, the light fixture in the shape of a spider candlestick holder. *Candelabra*, that was the word. *Pull out, you've got to pull out, pull out, fucking pull out, piece of shit*, and he did. He lowered himself, gripped his penis with one hand and one of my breasts with the other. He came right into my panties, letting his seed spill forth. He yowled into the air, his eyes closed, releasing himself to his own small world.

I mimed some chords of air guitar, sitting there on the bar stool across from Bordelon, letting my fingers strum wildly, committing to it. Bordelon laughed. She took out her gloss from her purse and rosed her lips within their lines. She offered the gloss to me. I put it on and smacked and tasted her Coke and fog and felt buzzy and blurry and light.

But in a minute she was back to thinking about what she was trying to forget.

Without any warning, she said to me, "I didn't want it."

"I know."

"Nobody did," she said.

"You may not have to keep it," I said. "You may still be able to decide."

"I'm too far along," she said. "I know it. It's done." She twisted the strap of her purse around her wrist.

I believed that a woman should choose, that Bordelon should have the right to choose. If she was past six weeks, and if she wanted to, she'd have to go to another state.

"Do you think you're past six weeks?"

"I haven't had my period in months, Alma."

That was when Cullen walked over to our table, thumped down two more drinks. This time, mine had a tiny red straw. I liked to chew on it when my drink was done.

"This round's on me," he said. "I'm Cullen, by the way."

"I know," I said.

"What's your name?" he said to Bordelon.

She looked down at the high-top table, chewed on her lip.

"Bordelon," she said quietly.

Then Cullen started talking, and didn't stop. He was going to LSU, pre-law. That was one of their biggest majors—that and business, accounting, atmospheric science, marine biology, agriculture, soil science. Himself? He was interested in environmental law, but if that didn't work out, then he'd do corporate. Something good for the world, or something to make money, he said. It would have to be one or the other. He'd make a decision soon. He said he was working at an ice-cream place during the semester, living in an apartment with four other guys. About those four guys, he said, they were two sets of twin brothers. Could you believe it? It was a three-bedroom place, and the two pairs of brothers shared the other two rooms. Wasn't that weird? Wasn't it obscene?

"Not in this economy," I said.

"Still think it's weird," he said. "Two sets of twins. I'm not making it up. They met at a twin convention." He put his hand to his heart. "Swear to God." He turned to Bordelon. "What do you think? Isn't it fucked-up, them all together like that?"

Bordelon was still twisting one of her purse straps around her wrist, making a loopy knot. She'd been quiet while he talked, looking at me or the TV.

"Hey," I said to Cullen. "We're just us, okay?"

"I know you're just you," he said.

"I mean," I said, "we're here to talk to each other. Me and her."

Cullen put his palms up in surrender. "Suit yourself," he said.

He walked behind the bar, started scooping out pebbled ice like diamonds into a bucket. On the TV, a Saint swigged Gatorade, watched his teammates tackle the Colts to shit. Bordelon let go of her purse, started to sip on her Coke. "Sweet Caroline" came blasting through the speakers. I danced a little with my shoulders. My second drink was half gone already.

"I don't even know nursery rhymes," she said.

"So what?"

"I can't even sing," she said. "You're supposed to sing to them."

"I can't sing worth shit," I said. "Sweet Caroline!" I sang in an ear-blistering wrong key.

"I'm serious," she said. "I've never held a baby."

I was trying to remember when I had. Once, when I'd gone with my mother to Our Lady of Perpetual Help, Celeste Blanchard had handed her mean baby to me. My mother called him a mean baby. Celeste didn't ask, just walked over after mass, plopped the squealing, runny-eyed baby in my arms. *Look at you*, she said. *You're a natural,* but Celeste knew nothing about me, and the mean baby kept crying out, knowing I was no natural.

Before "Caroline" was finished, Cullen was back, right there at Bordelon's elbow.

"My ears were burning over there," he said. "Were y'all talking about me?"

No, we weren't, I said.

Did we want another round? he said.

No, we did not.

Nobody asked him, but he pulled up a chair beside us, started back right where he'd left off, describing his apartment—no furniture, no TV, but there were some nice rugs and plants he'd bought, even a painting his mother had propped up against the wall, maybe he'd hang it up one day, right across from a mirror. I twirled my glass on the table, stared into the cyclone I made in my drink.

When he was done, I said, "Listen."

"Yeah?"

"I told you. We're just us right now." I pointed to Bordelon. "Me and her. Just us."

"Hey," said Cullen, putting his hands up again, as if that settled it. "I can take a hint."

"Apparently, you can't," said Bordelon. She was talking above the music, looking right at him, her eyes tinged with heat.

"We were talking," she said. "Talking privately. You know what that means?"

"Look, I wasn't coming to—" started Cullen. His birthmarks like islands began to blush.

"It means away from *you*," she said. "Away from you and anybody else. Not *to* you, not for you, and for fuck sure not about you." She turned to me. "Alma," she said, "let's go."

She stood up from the stool, holding her not-showing-anything-yet stomach while she slipped her feet to the floor. I took a last sip of my drink and stood up too.

"And don't pay the jackass," she said.

We left him sitting there, stunned and silent, letting the door slam behind us.

When we were back home, Bordelon took another bath, the bathroom door closed for hours, and I couldn't help it, I listened in on her mumbling and singing, something something something about the dog's run away with the spoon. And the cow and the fiddle, the cat and the middle, and the dish ran away with the moon.

The Cat Ran Away
with the Moon

I woke to the bleating call of a bird. I looked out my window to the backyard, scanned the grass. Birds seemed to sing less now, mostly sang before storms, but today was a rare cloudless day. I saw it in the distance, a muted gray blur pecking along the earth. I dug into my purse, found a package of two saltines. I opened my window, crumbled the crackers, threw the crumbs to the ground, watched the bird hop closer, mouth a crumb with her beak. I didn't know what kind she was. My mother would know, or Frances Boone. I closed the window, let the bird eat and bleat and be.

I smelled like shit and Four Roses, but I didn't shower or brush my teeth. I put on jeans, a black tank top, pulled my hair back with my mother's old barrette in the shape of a claw. I let Bordelon sleep, left her door closed, crept out the front, poured Purina out for lost Shane.

In the car, I turned up the AC and put on Alabama Shakes. August sun glazed the road. I drove to the library the short but windier way. I had things to do. I passed a row of shotgun homes, a little brick preschool, a penned-up colt in a field, standing in the clover. It was almost noon. The downstairs computer banks would be busy with the afternooners. Pegeen would be having her lunch at the desk, drinking something sugary for her hangover.

I was right. The computers were jammed with people watching cat videos or reading the news, and Pegeen was at her desk, about to bite into a sandwich, an uncapped bottle of Dr. Pepper beside her. Her eyes caught mine. She had eyes that saw everything. I wanted to speed upstairs, get to my research. Pegeen waved me over.

"Heard anything yet?"

"Turned in the letter yesterday," I said. "Too soon."

"Bastards," she said. "They're going to drag out the whole thing. That's what they do."

It looked like a pimento cheese sandwich, and I would have given her twenty dollars, if I'd even had a twenty on me, for half of it.

"Going upstairs," I told her.

"What are you doing up there?"

"I'll see you later."

"What's the secret upstairs?"

I pretended I didn't hear and jumped up the steps three at once, singing Alabama Shakes's "Always Alright" in my head. That was when I knew something in me was joyful—careful but surely joyful—holding on to light and feathery hope. If I had nothing else, I had that, which was more than I'd had in too long a time.

I logged on to the computer by the picture window upstairs—the field like a green sea underneath the cloudless sky—opened an incognito window on the screen. I searched with different words: *bury urn, burial, bury body, death care.*

I read about bodies. Several years earlier, some people had been doing natural burials. The body could go in a biodegradable casket or shroud, be reabsorbed into the earth. I read an article about a woman who, before mandated cremation, wanted to be absorbed into the earth as the roots of a tree. She was buried through a company called Of Ground, Of Soil, Of Earth: Natural Caskets and Burial, USA, Inc. I couldn't find their website.

Just for a moment I allowed myself to imagine my mother's body, her body as it had been when I last saw her, becoming the roots of a magnolia, and me there, asleep in the shade of its sinewy branches.

A year ago I'd gone to a psychic. I found her just outside St. Gen, in a pumpkin-colored cabin covered in vines. A neon sign, PALM READER, flashing in the window. I'd brought fifty in cash. She came out from behind a curtain, wearing a surgical mask, pulling an oxygen tank along with her. She was ill, she said through the mask, her heart didn't pump right. She said she should have died years ago; here she was, already living beyond what life should have given her.

Look at you, she said. *Just a baby, trying to find out the answers. Well,* she said, *babies need answers too.*

But she barely knew anything. She said I'd have a windfall soon, cold cash, but I'd have to work for it, be patient, put up with shit first. That was what my horoscope always said too: first comes shit, then maybe something righteous and good.

In two hours at the computer I couldn't find anything anywhere about illegal urn burial, not even a hint of blog or chat room talk. Not even an arrest for it in the entire country. There was illegal body burial, but nothing for an urn. Maybe the bastards were scrubbing it all out.

They may not float in the sea. They may not rise in the air. You may not scatter. You may not bury.

I would have to bury her urn on my own.

That palm reader took my money but never looked at my palm. That was the second worst money I ever spent. The worst was the hundred and fifty I lost to a slot machine on the *Betsy Ann* riverboat.

Bordelon, feet propped on the dash, her head tipped back, looked out the window at rain clouds bearing down. Wednesday morning. I was driving us to Marksville for her ultrasound. My brain felt fogged up from the humidity, like some shield of air or potent mist, invisible yet thick as a screen.

The night before, we'd been side by side on the couch, Bordelon's feet up on the coffee table, watching *Back to the Future II* on TV and eating Zapp's. She suddenly said to me, "They thought the future was hoverboards and fancy microwaves, but it wasn't. The future was *this*."

"What?"

"Climate change and dead people losing choices."

"And internet," I said. "TV and fucked-up attention spans."

"*Candy Crush.*"

"There was no predicting any of that shit," I said. "Their future's long gone for us, anyway."

In the movie, Marty McFly was being chased on a hoverboard.

"You'd think the government would allow people to choose what happens to their bodies after they die," Bordelon said. "Since they're so interested in protecting life."

"What, in the movie?"

"Not the movie. Now," she said. "Now!"

"They're not interested in protecting life," I said. "They just want to take away choices. Little by little."

That morning I'd been the one to call about the ultrasound. On the phone they'd said it was two hundred and forty dollars with no insurance. I made the appointment.

"I'll pay for part," I said to Bordelon.

"With what?" she said.

"My card."

"You put everything on that card," she said.

An unemployment check had come, a lucky stroke, my breezy windfall, and I needed to have my brake pads checked, but I didn't tell her. That would wait.

At the clinic, they took our money first. Eighty dollars from Bordelon in cash—from savings, she'd told me—and the rest on my Visa. The waiting room was empty, no coffee or TV, just a well-thumbed Bible on a scuffed wood table. She closed her eyes, pretended to sleep in the chair until a nurse called her back. I rose and walked behind Bordelon, put my hand on her shoulder. I could feel her trembling.

They brought us to an exam room, took her weight, made her pee in a cup, gave her a backless green hospital gown the color of mint gum, thin white paper like a big paper towel to wrap around her waist, told her to take off her underwear too. She went into a curtained-off corner of the room to change, came out in the gown and her pink flip-flops, her clothes in her arms.

"You want me to hold anything?" I said.

"I've got it," she said. She placed the pile on a chair, a pair of lavender panties on top. She stayed standing. Looked at the ultrasound equipment, a screen by the exam chair and another black screen up on the wall like a TV, a computer with a keyboard and mouse.

"Looks normal," I said, though it was my first time in a room like this. I'd seen things on TV. "Nothing hurts. It's painless."

"I know that," said Bordelon. She wouldn't look at me. She crawled up on the exam chair, wrapped the scratchy white paper around her, picked up a brochure on ectopic pregnancy, opened it, and stared.

The technician knocked and came in, introduced herself.

"My name's Milly," she said. She had on blue sneakers and scrubs that had a teddy bear pattern. Bordelon lifted her gown, her flip-flopped feet dangling off the chair.

"For this one," Milly said, "we're using a vaginal probe."

She held up a thick plastic wand, slightly curved.

"I thought you just needed my stomach," said Bordelon.

112

"We might be too early for that," said Milly. "We don't know."

"That goes inside me?" said Bordelon.

"Right."

"Looks like a penis," she said.

Milly inserted the probe. I watched the screen up on the wall, tried not to look at Bordelon. Then I heard her do a strange thing—she laughed, quick and loud and shrill.

"What does it feel like?" I said.

"You can guess," she said.

"Strange feeling, huh?" said Milly.

I said, "It's got to be strange the first time."

"Don't make jokes," said Bordelon. "Not now."

But then she laughed again, and she didn't stop laughing while the screen came on, started showing movement. I saw grainy shadows, the inside of Bordelon's womb like the inside of a cave. I didn't know what I was looking at.

"Looks dusty in there," Bordelon said, and that sent her to laughing again. I'd never heard such a strange laugh from her or anybody. "Sorry," she said. "I laugh when I don't know what to do."

"Hold on," said Milly. "I've got to look around."

Bordelon got quiet. In a minute, Milly went to the computer keyboard. She made a circle on the screen around something that looked like a pea pod with a head.

"There's Baby," she said.

She typed above the image of the pea pod on the screen: *Itty Bitty Baby.*

I looked back to Bordelon. She'd stopped laughing, was staring at the screen, an expression I couldn't read. I wanted to hold her hand, but her face told me she might pull away if I tried.

"Everything's looking okay," said Milly.

"Okay?" I said.

"Everything's looking good," said Milly.

Then she removed the vaginal probe, squeezed the gel over Bordelon's stomach, and put a device like a mouse over her stomach.

"We can do it this way now," said Milly.

She took some measurements. She checked for a heartbeat, told us to hold on. Then Milly said, "Heartbeat's good."

"You can hear it?" I said.

"You're at about sixteen weeks," Milly said to Bordelon. "I'm going off the measurements. Due date is January 22."

"Next year?" I said, as if I couldn't imagine it.

Bordelon wasn't saying a thing. I stared at the pea pod on the screen, watching the shadows bounce in her womb-cave.

"Girl or boy?" I said.

"Don't know yet," said Milly.

Milly printed out the picture on a little machine by the keyboard, smiled at the picture before she held it out to Bordelon. Bordelon sat there, staring past Milly as if she were dumbstruck. I reached out my hand, took the picture.

"For our album," I said, even though we had no such thing, and the picture might just curl up in the dark bottom of my purse.

"Later on, you can get better images," said Milly. "Three-D. Costs a few hundred more, but it's worth it."

Milly turned off the equipment, wished Bordelon luck, left the room. I turned to face her, at last. She wasn't moving. The white tissue paper was bunched up to her knees. She was still staring at the screen, with nothing there.

"How do you feel?" I said.

Her green gown was hanging off one shoulder, her lip gloss feathered at the corners of her mouth.

"I don't know," she said.

"Maybe California would let you at sixteen weeks," I said. "I don't know."

And she knew what I meant. Maybe it was too late for her to legally make a choice. A choice I thought she should have.

"How about California?" I said. "Do you want me to look it up?"

She didn't answer. She put a hand to her stomach.

"I'd drive you there," I said. "I'll look it up if you want me to."

She held her stomach. "Alma, don't ask me again," she said.

"All right," I said. "Okay. How are you?" I tried.

"Don't know," she said, but when she stayed sitting there and closed her eyes, tears fell thick and slow. She made no noise, just let them pearl down her face. I did not move or say a word. There was nothing I could say. I just watched her cry that way.

In silence we drove to St. Genevieve. As soon as I'd unlocked the front door, Bordelon was inside, walking to the bathroom. She turned on the tub faucet, closed the door. I shut myself in my mother's room, lay down in my mother's bed, took out my journal, my phone. I pressed record, aiming my phone camera right on me, reciting my own lines, filming myself for nobody.

> *"I could not think*
> *I could not love*

> *"Silence commemorates an exit*
> *better than an abrupt shriek*

> *"Within myself, a well*
> *isolate miracle*
> *in the foxfire wood the wren"*

If I remembered how I felt writing the words, letting the channels of my body open, I could cry. I could let myself. Sometimes I knew how to let myself. But tears wouldn't come. I heard Bordelon leave the bathroom, go to the living room, turn on an old sitcom on the TV, the laugh track ringing through.

> *"in the foxfire wood the wren*
> *quiets too*
> *with no one to sing for the bird"*

How could I let the words arrange themselves in my body? Open waves of sadness, let tears flood and follow. I waited for them, numerous or only a few. I felt my nose begin to run.

But then I saw my phone flash with blue, and my heart bumped. Here it was, sooner than I'd ever thought, a notification of an automated email from donotreply at the Office of the Parish Clerk. I could see the first line. *We regret to inform you.* I swiped to open.

We regret to inform you that you may not retain the ashes of the decedent.
This decision may not be appealed.

My mother, the email went on to say, was not my only next of kin. They'd found a record of my father, living in Wyoming. And there was more. I had two half brothers—my father had children with another woman, a Ms. Hallie Burstyn, also in Wyoming.

My mother's ashes, though she was the only family I knew, would be kept, gone from the living world, and away from me.

MARK THE PLACE

Within my body was a well, alive and simmering. And then it did happen—I cried in her bed. Three tears fell to my phone screen.

I had no interest in finding my father or my brothers, not even to search their names. Even alive, my father was more dead to me than anyone I knew.

It was already late afternoon. I turned over in bed. Through the window the sky was so pale it was nearly the color of the moon.

All I could do now was stare at the bedroom wallpaper, the violet buds, the jagged edges of the thistle, then upward to the pinwheeling ceiling fan, making slow, lazy turns, the shadow of an O as it spun. I counted the cycles. *Ten. Eleven. Twelve.* Josephine.

Josephine, I remembered, had wanted to know if I did not receive my mother's urn. I didn't know why. I had no phone number, only knew where she lived. I barely knew her, but I had no other choice. All I could do was go to her, tell her I was lost.

I left without waking Bordelon. She was asleep on the couch, her legs akimbo, one foot over the armrest, up against the curio. I made the drive to St. Francisville, not stopping. When I reached the fuchsia crepe myrtle, I slowed, let my eyes wander from the road. Like jewels, its leaves glowed darkly in the sun. More than a hundred degrees, but the tree seemed frozen. I'd once heard that of all the colors in the spectrum, the human eye could detect the most shades of green.

This time again, Josephine was at the door before I could knock, wearing her hair in a twist beneath her Tabasco hat, her rust-colored clogs and soil-stained jeans, her dime-size gold cross dangling in the hull of her throat.

"You've got some kind of radar?" I said.

"Heard you drive up," she said. "I hear everything here."

"I came to tell you," I said. "The clerk's office wrote back."

"What happened?"

"They didn't . . . didn't . . . they wouldn't."

Those were the only words I could get out, hoping something in her understood.

"I'll be damned," she said. "Come inside. You come with me."

Her menagerie of dolls watched as we passed through the living room. In the kitchen, she pulled out a rickety metal chair.

"Have a seat," she said.

She lit a blue candle that sat on the table, tall but thin as a finger. She sat across from me, closed her eyes for a moment, bowed her head. Then she fluttered her lids while her lips moved. I kept my eyes open and on the scar that crosshatched her top lip, traveled down to her chin in the curved shape of a C.

"Are we having a séance?" I said, though I knew she was saying a prayer.

She opened her eyes—those blue starling-egg eyes—and looked right at me. I felt stunned for a moment, a bright thrum leaping through to my own eyes. I could hear the clock ticking in the other room.

"I'll get you something to drink," she said, standing, breaking the spell of whatever had just happened. "Sounds to me like you need it." She brought out a pitcher of orange juice from the refrigerator, took down two small glasses from a cabinet.

"You told me to come see you," I said. "So I'm here."

"Because I wanted to know," she said. "If they didn't give back your mother."

"Well, I'm here," I said impatiently. "Are we just going to pray?"

"And other things," she said.

"And?"

"I know people," she said. She set the glasses on the table, poured out the juice. "I know somebody who can help."

"Who?"

"I can't say," she said.

"Can't say why?"

"Somebody particular."

"Well. Tell this *somebody particular*, I don't have any money."

I looked to the finger-thin candle, embarrassed. The flame had gone out without my noticing. Josephine said she wasn't asking for money, she wasn't asking for anything. Well, one thing, she said. I kept my eyes on the burnt candlewick.

"What?" I said.

"I just ask for a little time," she said. "Patience. How are you with patience?"

"I can work on it," I said.

From her pocket she brought out her same pair of crinkled garden gloves, webbed and laced with dark stains of earth.

"Want to help me?" she said.

"In the garden?"

"Only if you want," she said. "Helps with patience too."

"And then what?" I said. "You'll help me with the urn?"

"It's not a trade," she said. "Just help if you want. Unless you have something to get back to."

What I had to get back to was staring at the bedroom wallpaper, counting the dings and rips in the thistles, waiting for Bordelon to wake or the day to pass so I might sleep and wake to another day and night gone, a little more time passed, like another bead on a string, and I could hope to miss my mother a little less.

"I can help," I told her.

* * *

We began with the weeds, rank and wild. They were knotted in great clumps all around the seedlings and sprouts.

"I let the weeds grow," said Josephine. She pulled on her gloves, tugged the brim of her Tabasco cap low on her head, and knelt down. "We'll get them. But leave some in there. I always leave some in."

I didn't ask why. I knew at least one reason—they were weeds, but delicate. Weeds, but pretty and spangled with color. Star-shaped, tiny blooms lolled on their stems. What was the difference between weed and flower? These weeds tangled and rolled, like shapes of green brains and briar.

She reached out, gripped a long stem by its neck. She yanked, tearing the weed straight from the soil. If the weed could have screamed, I believe it would have. She moved on to the head of a snarled weed clump, ripped the bunch from the ground with a single snap. I could hear them break from the earth.

"Come on," she said. "Help me."

She did not look up. She moved to the next batch, steadying herself on her knees, ready to rip the sleek stems.

"Come," she said.

I knelt beside her, chose a weed bunch, wrapped my hand there as if to strangle. And I strangled, I pulled up, I tore. Their roots like a thick nest, their leaves warm and bristled. We discarded to the right, moved to the left. Pulled and grabbed and snatched and seized. I pretended my hand was a mouth, and down the mouth came, open and ready, biting each weed from the ground.

"To pray," said Josephine, "is to hope. To ask. To ask and wonder. What do you want to ask?" She did not look up. She tore at a tough stem violently. "You don't have to say it out loud. You can ask without using words."

I said nothing. It was as though I were asking something of the world without exactly knowing the words or what it was. A tendril of moss wormed its gray way around a flowering weed. At the center of the petals, the heart of the flower sat like a gold eye. I almost left it there. But the garden's sprouts were overrun, would need to grow. I snapped the head of the flower clean from the stem.

Josephine stopped, looked to me. "Good," she said. "Very good. Keep going now. Keep asking."

I sat up on my knees, pulled back my hair with a rubber band from my pocket. I scratched my nose with the heel of my hand. The pinwheel was right there, turning in the hot wind. I bent back down to work beside Josephine. I was asking, asking, weeding, ripping, feeling my asking becoming a new thing, becoming anger.

I moved farther, I moved faster. My hands clearing, attacking. Sprouts from the seeds we'd planted were more and more visible, like stars opening, brightening. I clawed and shredded, suddenly bursting, splitting the stems. And then, without thinking, I bent down to the ground, opened my mouth, bit the pink flowering head of a weed from its stem with my teeth. I tasted earth. I tongued and teethed the texture of petal and bloom and soft lips.

Josephine turned, watched me as I chewed the flower. Then she opened her mouth wide and laughed—the scar above her lip trembling—a full-hearted laugh, the best I'd ever heard.

I swallowed the flower, buried it in my body.

"Come with me," said Josephine. She stood with some difficulty, her knees crackling. She went to a little table she kept in the yard and picked up two garden spades. She handed one to me, bronzed with rust, the shape of a tongue. She led me to the edge of the yard, to a tree stump striped with beads of fungus. She held her spade up over her head. Then, in a blur, she brought the spade down on the stump with a solid clang.

"Holy shit," I said.

"It's good for you," she said, wiping sweat from the back of her neck. "Releases energy."

She brought her spade up again, hit the tree stump square on the bulbs of fungus.

"Go to it," she told me. "Hit as much as you want."

"You could break the shovel."

"Nevertheless," she said.

She brought up her spade, hit the stump with an even stronger blow.

"I do it all the time."

She gave another hit, letting out a tremendous breath. "All the time," she told me. "Go to it."

I raised my spade in the air, opened my eyes wide, gave a short yell. I brought the spade down, clanging it on the stump, the sound of the hit soaring, loud and clean.

I was home before dusk, the sky stung with deep pink. In the carport, there was Shane, waiting. The other cats sang in a chorus, asking for food, and Shane stood in the center like a star. She lapped her coarse tongue at my ankles, her shaggy mane scruffy and full. I felt her body for any sores or bruises. From what I could tell, she was just as she'd been when she left. I scooped out Purina on paper plates, an extra plate for the prodigal Shane.

Inside, the house was dark and quiet, not even the TV flickering. I was dirty with the earth, sweating between my toes and under my breasts. I switched on the living room light, the ceiling fan, no Bordelon. The bedroom door was closed. I looked back to the sofa, the coffee table crammed with empty sleeves of crackers, *Star* and *People* magazines.

I walked out to the mailbox. When the mail had no check, there were only throwaways—bills and forms and nothing flyers for politicians and insurance—but sometimes there was another windfall. My mother had paid money into some kind of teacher's government fund, and every now and then a bit of it came to me. I never knew how much it would be or when it'd come, but I knew it by sight, that gorgeous slip of a check, stiff in its envelope.

There was no check. Only a couple of bills, and beneath those, an official envelope from the Office of the Parish Clerk, long and slim. I went inside, tore the head of the envelope clean off. It was the same as what they'd said in their email—I would not receive the decedent's ashes, BROUS440931—signed by the parish clerk, signed again by some other government overpaid so-and-so phony, and sealed. *Please keep this for your records.*

I tore the letter to smithereens. I opened the front door and scattered the paper bits to the air. I shut the door before the bits could land.

"Here," I said, "are my *fuck-you* records."

In my mother's room, at the sagging center of the bed, I sat with my dull graphite pencil, my drawing pad laid on my crossed knees. Here was the crest of her forehead, her eyes flecked with light, the bare tree of veins at her temple. I kept a rhythm, my pencil barely lifting, a song to the sound of the lead across paper. The jaw that softly veed to her chin. I was drawing my mother's face from memory.

My best photo of her was still in my leather portfolio on the floor of my room. I'd never put away the papers. To myself, I called the photo the Pearl-Eye Picture. Her face was only half in frame, cut off at the edge. There was the fanned wave of her hair, a delicate ear, and one blue, pearled eye. I took it out only rarely. I could never look at it long. You could not simply sit and stare at a Book of Spells.

I went back to Josephine's garden. Again and again, over the weeks, I'd return to it. In the morning I'd scan job ads on my phone, apply where I could—Home Depot in Alexandria, Piggly Wiggly in Marksville—and then there I'd be, driving to St. Francisville, each time passing the roadside crepe myrtle that glowed fuchsia. Sometimes I imagined it as a many-winged animal, the thick branches tiering upward.

Bordelon did not come with me. Too exhausted, she said, and anyway, she'd read online that pregnant women weren't supposed to garden. Stay away from soil and cat litter, she'd read. Something about toxins and parasites.

She'd sleep and snore past the morning on the couch, eat snacks I'd bring her, turn the TV on and let it run. She'd pull the diamonded quilt up to her chin, lean back into the pitiful couch cushions, nap, wake, and watch endless shows of house renovations, *Price Is Right, Law & Order,* sitcoms of families in two-story homes I didn't know how anyone afforded.

Her belly—her whole body—swelled. She let her belly lead as she walked through the house, her feet puffed up, her ankles growing redder and rounder. She said everything about her felt as though it were ripening.

"You have no idea," she loved to say to me, "what this feels like."

"Never said I did," I said.

"None."

"Can you feel it kick? Or tumbling over?"

"Sometimes, sure. Like at night. If I'm sitting still, if I'm eating sugar. It loves sugar. He loves sugar."

She touched her hand to her stomach. I didn't know why, but I wanted to touch it too. But she never told me I could place my own hand there. I did not ask, only imagined the drumlike skin of her stomach, the baby's foot as if on the other side of a wall.

She told me she wasn't going back to the clinic. Too much fuss, too expensive. Women had been having children without checkups and ultrasounds for centuries. The Alexandria hospital, she told me, had its own program. A doctor there delivered babies for women without insurance for under seven hundred, and she could do that if she cleaned out a savings account from her grandmother and started working right after the baby, and that's where we would go—if I'd take her—to Alexandria.

"Of course I'll take you," I said.

"And I'm going to ask for as many drugs as I can pay for."

"Pray for?"

"Pay for."

And she would stay here at the house with me, with the baby, for a week, maybe, no longer than two, just that, and when she healed, she'd drive to Opelousas to see Fuck.

I asked her what she'd need, diapers or a blanket or a swinging crib. I could find used things at church sales, garage sales. People would help us. But she said she wanted nothing. Online, she bought more prenatal vitamins, the expensive kind, two pairs of large pants she could grow into. She rationed the vitamins. I helped her split each pill with a bread knife—just half of one a day.

But silently, slowly, we were agreeing to leave each other to ourselves. I wasn't sure how that had started. Her pregnant stomach was some unspoken division between us. *You have no idea what this feels like.* I knew I probably never would. I wanted no child of my own. If a person lost choices—even of how they wanted to die—maybe they weren't really your child. Maybe they didn't even belong to themselves.

I could not keep away from the garden. Each time, Josephine welcomed me back. We'd weed and shear, hack and rip, in rain or no rain. Muddying ourselves in the darkened earth, digging up clots of soil, protecting our sprouts, their thin root systems forming like the shape of brains. Josephine would tighten her gloves around her wrists, pull down her Tabasco hat over her starling-egg-blue eyes.

"Here," she told me. "You'll need these."

She held out a stained, scruffed cap with PAPA'S PIZZA in block letters, and a bright pair of lime-green gardening gloves.

"For you," she said.

The very best thing I liked to do was fill the oversize watering can to the brim. I'd turn on the hose, set its long neck down into the can's plastic well, wait for the water to fill, think or sing to myself while the water ran. *Body, be still. Nerves, now rest.* Simple, the water rising to the top.

Too much rain in September hurt us. We were doing an impossible thing. We'd plant, and a storm would take our sprouts. We'd plant, and more rain would come. The ground stayed wet even on sunlit days. Josephine raised a blue tarp over our rows, said some prayers over our sprouts.

"I'm asking," she began, "that you protect them. Protect them, Lord."

She bowed her head for a long, heart-stopping time. Then I had to ask her, the big thing on my mind.

"Have you talked to the person you know?" I said. "That somebody particular? About my mother?"

"I have," she said.

"And? And what?"

"Be patient."

She bowed her head. I'd stay quiet, look skyward.

That was the day when Josephine started to talk about Mandy. It began with how Mandy used to dig through the soil, unearthing beetles and worms, then tromp through the house with her caked paws and dripping nose. Mandy, a honey-hearted collie-something and something and something else, Josephine never knew what she was. She'd gotten her at the pound—the orphanage, she called it.

"She's dead now?" I said.

"She's in Denham Springs," she said.

"What's she doing there?"

"Living with my ex."

I stopped, looked up from my weeding. It was a rare rainless day. The ground had dried quickly. Josephine was crouched beside me, picking at a newborn petal.

"My ex-husband," she said again. "Frank. But Mandy was mine."

"What's she doing with him?"

"He gets what he wants."

She sat back on the ground then, groaned softly. "My *knees*," she said. "Getting old is good. I happen to like it. But these *knees*." She took off her cap. Her hair had stayed neat and coiled, like a small gray wreath on top of her head.

Then she told me—she'd been a schoolteacher there, in Denham Springs, third grade. She'd adored it—that was the word she'd used, *adored*—she'd been happy on her own, for years like that, not wanting any children, but wanting to teach other people's. When she met Frank, she'd been happy too. She'd met him through a friend. He was nice, chivalrous at first—buying her roses in baby's breath, taking her out for seafood dinners, trips to the beach—and then he wasn't.

"One day," she said, "he got a different kind of angry. He grabbed my wrist. The next time he was angry, he grabbed my throat. Next time, he went for my mouth."

For a while Frank stopped, found AA, found Jesus, found God. Between the two of them, he was the one to find Jesus first. Then there was dancing, the movies, the beach. She remembered why she'd started with him.

"Then he changed again," she said.

She leaned closer to me, put her finger inside her mouth. She peeled her lip back, put her face near mine. She wanted me to look. What I saw was this: puckered skin, scars in the shapes of circles and dashed lines, white, pulpy scars where pink flesh should be. Taking her finger away, she closed her mouth.

"Cigarettes," she said. "His cigarettes."

"He burned you?" I said.

She nodded.

"Fuck," I said. "Fuck."

"If he'd be in the wrong mood," she said. "He'd smoke one, then another, and then he'd start in. Afterward, I'd lock myself in the bathroom. I'd fall asleep in there. On the floor sometimes. All I would do was wish I could be somewhere else. I spent hours wishing that. Please, please, let me be anywhere else. Let me."

Her blue starling-egg eyes were wide with sadness, remembering. I wondered how long it had been since she'd told the story.

"And so I left," she said. "I moved here."

She'd first been in St. Genevieve when she was a child. She was with her family—her parents, a toddler brother—visiting an uncle. They'd spent the day at the water. She laid in the sun next to her mother, who wore a wide-brimmed straw hat. She remembered that hat, her brother dozing in her mother's arms. Her father and uncle had spent the day trying to fish. Josephine had fallen asleep next to the sound of the lisping water, the sun moving limply over her body. It had been a perfect day, one she'd always thought about.

"I came here," she said. "Gave up Mandy. Started over."

"Well, damn it all," I said.

"And I realized," she said, "who I was talking to in that bathroom. Who I was talking to when I asked to be somewhere else, anywhere else."

I didn't ask who. I knew who she'd say.

"I wish you'd come to church with me sometime," she said. "Come to St. Francis Xavier."

"Maybe," I said.

"You need to come," she said. "Come to church. Stay humble, stay light."

I didn't ask her what she meant by that. I knew she wanted me to ask, and I didn't.

I stayed there until dusk, filling the watering can, carrying it back and forth from the hose to the garden, the water sloshing and frothing. There wouldn't be rain the next day, and the sprouts would be thirsty. The yard pinwheel slowed in the wind, but the tinny wind chimes picked up speed and sang.

In my head, I cursed Frank.

I tilted the can, showered our sprouts, giving each one its due, counting to ten, moving down the row, tilting the can again, feeling the stream and plash of the water. Each time I tilted the can—I cursed Frank. And when I got to the count's end—*nine, ten*—I cursed Frank. I cursed Frank. I cursed Frank.

I refilled the can, laying the hose's long neck over the rim, letting its little mouth spill out, replenish the well. Better than I ever had, I could hear the lapping of the water against the can, the pooling, the droplets gathering. The water sputtering, pluming forward.

The lamp on the side of the house switched on, and when I walked through the darkening yard to the garden carrying the full watering can, Josephine was no longer there. She was just a few feet away, barefoot now, her clogs off and flipped over in the grass. She'd taken down her hair, the whole flood of gray now fallen to her elbows. She was watchful, staring ahead, following fireflies that picked along in the dark.

OCTOBER

The air thinned. The bright green—still green, always green—was fading. Mist rose from the ground in the early morning, slipped in the grass and weeds of my overgrown yard.

I'd started to stay up through the night. Writing, drinking, drawing. Lines and scraps and scrawls through swigs of Alberta Rye or George Dickel. But as I drew and wrote, I knew I would let it all go. In the morning I gathered all the paper, tore it to strips and bits and crumbs. I kept nothing, nothing, except for the one drawing I'd done of my mother. I was drawing better than I ever had, maybe because I knew I'd throw it all away. I liked making things that I knew would not stay in this world. Then I could write or draw what I wanted. There would be no trace of me.

On the other side of the wall, Bordelon snored through her dreams. She told me she'd felt the baby flutter and twist. Sometimes its kicks pained her, and she'd jump from the couch with a yelp.

"Hey!" she'd say, her hand to her stomach. "Hey, quit that. Quiet down in there."

I still did not touch, did not ask to touch, just watched her stomach plump, her legs thicken, her breasts grow round and pear. But her face and arms—they did not change. Only from her chest down could you know that something was growing inside her, eating each thing she ate, breathing what she breathed.

What she ate was Skittles and Chips Ahoy and half vitamins and scrambled eggs and Zapp's barbecue and Blue Bell butter pecan and Bugles. I gave her no advice. I did not know, she reminded me, would not ever know, what this felt like.

Each time I saw her now, Josephine would ask—could I come to St. Francis Xavier? Maybe this week I'd come to St. Francis Xavier. They were having a youth lock-in at St. Francis Xavier. A choral concert at St. Francis Xavier.

One afternoon, when I was just waiting for her to mention the latest attraction at St. Francis Xavier, she handed me a gleaming new shovel, taller than me, for the compost we'd started. She showed me how to scoop and turn the pile, scoop and turn. My legs hurt from bending. I could feel the metal hum and vibrate and sing. I dug in and turned the gummed clumps of soil. The coffee grounds, vegetable peels, eggshells, bird feathers, small cyclones of hair. Worms curled and rolled underneath.

"You need to come to church," Josephine started again. She stood beside me, watching me as I scooped and turned. "Stay humble, stay light."

I didn't feel light. I dug in the compost with the shovel, leaning down low in my knees, bearing the heft, smelling the stink of the dazzling muck. I was drunk on the smell of the dizzying, drummed-up earth.

"Maybe," I said. "Sometime."

"This time," she said. "I'm asking you specially to come. It's to see somebody."

"What somebody?"

"You know."

"Who?"

"*Somebody*," she said. "That somebody particular."

I stopped, the shovel still in the air, looked at Josephine.

"A parishioner," she said. "They're going to help you with your mother."

"Could you tell me who it is?"

"Just come," she said. "Come with me to church."

"They have to meet us there? That's the only place?"

I didn't like being tricked into church. It had happened to me before. Simple things—a girl in fourth grade inviting me for a movie night that began with popcorn but ended with Bible study. In high school, a slumber party that my mother forced me into, which turned into a youth retreat. Josephine's face looked real to me, sincere and hoping.

"The only place," said Josephine. "You'll come?"

I told her then that I would. I told her it would be for my mother.

"Just once," I said. "The one time."

"One time," said Josephine. "I'll take that." She took the shovel from me, started turning the compost herself.

That night, I told Bordelon, asked her to come with me for company, but she didn't want any part of it.

"You know what they're going to say to an unmarried pregnant girl in church?" she said. "A *teenager*? No, thanks. They'd never let me leave without confessing my sins. No, thank you." She pulled the quilt around her, turned up the volume on the ladies selling holiday cookie cutters on QVC.

"And don't pray for me," she said. "Don't you dare pray for me."

What I would pray for, or simply think to myself—ask for, ask of the air, or spirit, or those who had died before me who ever loved me or might still feel love toward me, or God, or whatever I could call it, I didn't know—I didn't know, I didn't know.

With my mother, I'd gone to Our Lady of Perpetual Help for midnight mass on Christmas Eve, stood and kneeled and sat and kneeled again, followed what my mother did. I remembered her long, beautiful hands folding and wrapping themselves together in prayer. I waited in the pew while my mother stood in line to take Communion and wine, the priest placing the wafer on her tongue, giving her the cup to sip, wiping the cup's lip after she drank.

What did the wafer taste like? I asked after.
The flesh of the Lord, she said.
What's that like?
Like bread.

And the wine?

Like grape juice, she said. *It's real. It's the blood of the Lord.*

For Christmas Eve, the church was dark, the Advent wreath above the altar a halo of four candles, the air dusky with incense. On the crucifix at the front of the church, a plaster Jesus wore his thorned crown, his thick-boned feet and palms nailed to the cross, his side bleeding. Each year I returned, the red paint on his torso had faded. His eyes were closed in agony. He did not look like a man to me. He looked like a boy, and all I could think of was how a child could go through so much pain.

When I fell asleep, my mother would touch my elbow gently, whisper my name. *Alma. The priest is praying. Listen. The priest is singing.*

Josephine had asked me to be there on Wednesday. On my way, I recited what I could remember of the Our Father, the Hail Mary, the Nicene Creed. *The seen and unseen. The living and the dead. And his kingdom shall have no end.*

Outside the church, Josephine was waiting. I saw her as I drove up, parked my car in the small lot. Her hair was down and combed to a shine. She wore a long dress the color of milk.

We were alone. "Come in," she said. "Come with me."

I'd put on my longest, most uncomfortable dress, black and loose, with thin straps. One I would have worn to a funeral.

We entered through the back. She led me up the center aisle, cutting through rows of pews made of pale wood.

At the front of the church, in front of the altar placed on a small stage, she paused and knelt, crossed herself, then stood again.

"Do you want me to do that?" I said.

"Do what you want," she said. "I won't make you do anything."

I stayed standing, bowed my head, closed my eyes. When I looked up, there was the figure of Jesus nailed to the crucifix, his eyes open, eyes to the sky, arms spread wide like the wings of a bird. This Jesus did not look like a boy to me now.

"Come with me," said Josephine. "I need your help. Back here."

"I thought you were introducing me to someone," I said.

"They're in here."

I followed her up a few carpeted steps, up on the stage, passing the altar. I'd never been so close to the crucifix, the altar with a thick white cloth laid over its surface, the tabernacle. She took my hand.

"This way," she said.

She led me to a small, round door to the left of the altar, turned the knob with a few clicks. I realized I was barely breathing. I felt we were entering a tomb.

Inside, the room was plain, ordinary. Josephine turned on a fluorescent light. The priest's long robes hung from a wheeled metal clothes rack. Binders and notebooks lay on a card table, a metal folding chair with ST. FRANCIS XAVIER stamped on its back. In the corner, a music stand overflowed with curled pages of sheet music. There was a

140

small, square sink, a round mirror, a few wood cabinets. We were in the sacristy, Josephine said.

"Here," she said. "I need your help."

She pulled the metal folding chair across the floor, to the cabinets beside the sink.

"I need something in there," she said.

She pointed up to the highest, tiny cabinet, the little white knob like an eye. I stepped up onto the chair, steadying myself on Josephine's shoulder as I did, and reached up, opened the cabinet.

There, inside, sitting in the center, was something I didn't recognize. I looked closer. Silver, pear-shaped, reflecting the light. Smooth metal. It sat there like some alien shape, an object from another world. An urn.

"Take it," said Josephine. She was staring up at me, her face so close I felt her breath on my elbow.

My hands shook. I picked up the urn, took it out into the light. A label with the quick response code was on the front, with a number beneath it. BROUS440931.

It was her.

I lost my balance on the folding chair.

"Come down from there," said Josephine. She pulled at my elbow, helped me step down to the floor. I looked at my mother's urn again, then cradled it to me.

"Is this real?" I said.

"Of course it's real," she said.

"This is her?" I said. "How?"

I stared at the urn in my hands, factory-sealed and government-issued, the metal as smooth and cool as a bell, my mother, my mother, my mother.

Then Josephine went quickly. She opened a cabinet, took out plastic grocery bags, a white and red canvas tote that said ALE RIVER in faded red letters. She swaddled the urn in the grocery bags, placed it all neatly in the canvas tote.

"Bring it home and keep it there," she said. "Don't let anybody see it. Nobody."

I couldn't believe any of this was happening. Josephine hooked the strap of the Ale River tote around my shoulder, led me from the sacristy, past the altar, down the center aisle cutting the pews, out to my car. I opened my trunk. We tucked the tote at the very back.

"Now go straight home," said Josephine.

"Are you going to tell me how you did this?" I said.

She looked to her right, and I followed her eyes. Someone was sitting in the driver's seat of a parked sedan. I looked closer. I knew the face. I remembered. It was the round-faced, red-cheeked woman I'd seen at the Office of the Parish Clerk. She smiled at me through the car window.

"Jennifer's a parishioner," said Josephine.

"Jennifer," I repeated.

"You can't tell anybody. Just I know, and Jennifer, Father Malcolm, and that's all. That's how you have to keep it, hear me?"

"You've done this before?" I said.

She didn't answer.

"Where did they go?" I said.

"They were buried."

Past the parking lot, I saw only the church, and one other small, windowless building that looked like a shed.

"Buried where?" I said. "Here?"

"We have a place," she said. "Not here. A long way away."

"Where?"

"Don't you worry about it."

I asked if I owed any money to anyone. Or anything. Anything to anybody, I'd find a way to pay it. What did I owe?

"Of course not," said Josephine. "You don't owe us a thing."

I flew the whole road home. Bordelon woke to the sound of the door, her face flushed with dream.

"How's God doing?" she said.

I kept walking. I could hear a rerun of *Naked and Afraid* playing on the TV, survivalists trying to build a fire in the rain. I knew that episode. The woman got frostbite on Day 3.

"He's fine, just fine," I said. "He says hello."

"How were the Jesus people?" she said.

"They still love Jesus," I said.

"Some things never change."

"Go back to sleep."

"Are those snacks in your bag?" she asked. "Snacks would be plum."

"Go to sleep. It's about to rain." I knew she loved to sleep in the rain.

"Maybe the lights will go out," she said.

In my room I laid the Ale River tote on the bed, delicately unwrapped the nest of plastic bags and uncovered the urn. BROUS440931. *Naomi.*

With both hands I picked up the urn, curled my fingers around its curves. It smelled like dull metal, and that was all. I had the strange thought to shake it, to know for certain my mother's ashes were inside. But I did not. I held it still, felt its weight in my hands, lighter than I ever imagined.

I'd read that the urns were sealed by machines, mechanical arms like the necks of long dragons, but I still tried what I knew I could not do—I placed my hand on the lid and twisted. I wiped the sweat on my hand on the skirt of my dress, twisted again, harder. It would not open. It would not move.

I rubbed my fingers over the quick response code, the size of a child's thumbprint. I put the urn to my cheekbone, felt the metal against my skin, the cool surface against me, the tingle and prick. And how could this, only this, be the weight of her? Her whole body contained in this.

Where would I put her? I took another long look at the urn, wrapped it in the Ale River tote, opened my bedside drawer, and gently laid it there. She would be there, *here*, *here*, next to me.

About the Pearl-Eye Picture—my mother told me about it once. She was thirty. She was looking back at her mother, who was behind the camera. She loved her mother. What you could not see, my mother told me, was her glass of champagne, a corsage pinned to her dress.

Expensive champagne, crisp corsage. It was some event, some occasion. A birthday, a wedding, a holiday. What she remembered was her happiness. She told me she'd felt it in her whole body. Coming up through her feet, up through the top of her head. Radiating through her like a source. You don't forget happiness like that. In a couple of months, she said, she'd be pregnant with me.

NEVERTHELESS

When she was alive, my mother had few wishes, and so far I had only gone against one. Her wishes—that I'd go with her to church on Christmas Eve, finish high school, find a summer job at sixteen, and not fall in with the smokers and misfits and cutups. My first job was at seventeen, one June, answering phones and sorting mail at a lawyer's office. I kept a handheld fan on my desk, taking off my polyester blazer when I was alone, sitting in the air-conditioning with only my tank top on, running my fan over my chest. And for a little bit that summer too, I fell in with Tristan, a blue-eyed cutup. My mother never knew that, just as she did not know I bummed two Pall Malls at a seventh-grade pep rally and smoked my way through freshman free period, hiding out in the bathroom stall by the open window, listening to Duck, Duck, Goose and Red Rover and *I've got a boyfriend and he said stop* from the kids in the catty-corner playground.

* * *

Burying her in my drawer was not burying her in the earth. The first night, I did not sleep. I drew, I drank, I wrote a few loose, scraggly lines of a poem—*a shroud of fire blooms, a stalk of ice in the field*—I left the drawer alone, did not look at the urn all night. If I looked, I would worry that it would be taken from me. Beautiful things, things hard to be believed, couldn't be looked at for long.

On the third day, I could not let it alone. All I could think of was the urn, abandoned in the drawer. I had to honor my mother's wish. I could not keep her body preserved, as she'd wanted, but I knew I could bury her. I could still give her that.

The yard was grown over with wild grass and weeds as thick as hair. I'd mowed it many times. There was a rectangle that was shady even in summer, just large enough to seal my mother's urn within the earth. I'd have to dig at night, hope for no rain.

I made plans. Online, I bought my own shovel, my own gloves, a headlamp. I watched the weather, hoped for no rain, hoped for supple, givable ground.

On a half-moon night, just after rain, it was time. I waited until Bordelon had fallen asleep on the sofa. I put on my headlamp, my gloves, crept out the back—with my shovel and my mother's urn in the Ale River tote—to the starlit slice of earth. The night was Louisiana October cold, the air muggy and fragrant. Beside my grandfather's bench, I cleared the patch of ground, furred with grass and capped with wispy blossoms.

I raised my shovel above my head, counted to five.

Then I brought the shovel down. I struck the ground as hard as my muscles would allow.

But the ground would not give. I tried to push the tip of the shovel into the earth, leaning with all my weight. The ground would not break.

I brought my shovel up, struck the ground again. The clang sang out through the night. I struck again, again, again, feeling the shovel shake in my hands as I pounded the solid earth. I might as well have been pounding against the sky.

I switched off my headlamp and sat for a while, let my muscles rest. Mist weaved through the grass, found pockets in the ground. I listened to the silence, thought of wildflowers popping and budding and sprouting invisibly in the dark, ready to burst and stun the world. The clear sky showed the stars. I'd seen on the news that there'd been a spike in people buying up stars, naming them after dead loved ones. I wondered what a star cost. I was staring up into memorials.

I stood again, raised the shovel over my head, brought it down with a zing on the ground.

"God damn, Alma."

I jumped and looked to my left. Bordelon stood there in a shirt to her knees, barefoot in the grass.

"You fucking scared me," I said.

"You fucking scared *me*," she said. "I know what you're doing." She looked at the tote on the ground.

"How in hell do you know that?" I dropped the shovel, pulled the bottom of my shirt up to my forehead, and wiped my temples.

"Well, I don't know everything," she said.

"What do you know?"

"I know you're burying her," she said.

I was relieved. I didn't want to keep such a thing from Bordelon. She was the only person I had to tell things to. I felt my body relax.

"You can't tell anyone," I said.

"Of course I won't," she said. "And I don't have any-body to tell."

"Even so," I said.

Bordelon touched her stomach through her shirt, rubbed toward her belly button. I still had not felt her stomach, had not felt the twists and turns of the baby's body, warm and incubated like a little hatchling. But Bordelon was shivering in the cold.

"My feet are frozen," she said.

"Sit down." My grandfather's bench was dewy and dirt-stained, but I pointed to it, and she sat, stretched her shirt over her knees, and hugged her knees to her chest.

"Come on," she said. "No one cares if you're burying an animal."

"An animal?"

"Cats are okay to bury."

"*Cats?*"

"Shane," she said. "Shane's in that bag?"

"My god," I said. "This is my mother."

I picked up the tote from the ground, brought out the urn, held it up for Bordelon to see.

"This is my mother," I said. "Naomi."

Bordelon stood up from the bench, her eyes on the urn. I could hear her breathe in the dark. She looked at the metal shining in the icy brightness of the moonlight.

"Can I touch it?" she said. "Her?"

"Yes," I said. "Naomi."

She did not hold the urn, but stretched her hand over its surface, letting her fingers glide across the metal. I knew just how it felt beneath her hand.

"How did you get it?" she said. "Her? Naomi?"

I told Bordelon about St. Francis Xavier, the altar, the sacristy, how Josephine had helped me, given me the ashes, told me the urn was mine. Now I had to bury it, and I told her why.

I turned on my headlamp. I gave the urn to Bordelon to hold, told her to stand back. I raised the shovel above my head, struck the ground with my mightiest blow, but I felt no give, no move, no crack in the earth. I inspected the ground. Maybe I'd made a shallow ding, just the size of a mouth. I let out a breath I didn't know I'd been holding, my breathing visible in the air.

"Not much," I said.

Bordelon held my mother's urn to her chest, looked down to the ground that would not break.

"Nothing," she said.

"The ground's not like this at Josephine's."

"It's a sign," said Bordelon.

151

"Give me some time."

"It's a sign," she said.

"It's no sign," I said.

"It's a sign, it's a sign. You can't bury her here."

I held the shovel above my head.

"Nevertheless," I said, and struck the ground again.

NEVADA

I imagined casinos studding the flat, ruddy desert. I imagined everyone thirsty, tongues lolling from their mouths. I imagined the ground so hot you could not walk.

St. Francis Xavier kept an illegal graveyard outside of Boulder City, Nevada. The ground in my own yard would not give beneath my shovel, though I'd tried for most of the night. I'd made a few marks in the earth, some nothing dents, and that was all the ground would give.

I went to Josephine the next morning, sat with her on her stiff floral sofa in the living room, something we'd never done. All her dolls stayed perfectly still and watched us through their glass.

I told it to her plainly. That my mother wanted to be buried in the ground, that I wanted to give this to her, her own wish, and that my yard was not the place.

"What about yours?" I asked.

She shook her head. "Not here," she said.

"Your ground's soft. Your soil comes up like that."

"Not here, we can't," she said. "But there is a place."

"What place?"

"The church has got one," she said.

She told me the graveyard was in Nevada. It did not belong just to St. Francis Xavier. A group of churches owned it, a network of God's people breaking the law. She didn't know how big the graveyard was or how many bodies were buried, but there was space. There was no worry about that. She said she thought we could make the drive in four days, even three. Father Malcolm had already given his blessing, though I'd never met the man or asked for any blessing. It was as if she'd known I'd come to her.

I wouldn't leave Bordelon behind, and Bordelon said that, anyway, of course she wanted to come. We locked up the house, got into the car. In the backseat footwell we put my zippered duffel, and inside that I'd swaddled my mother's urn in the Ale River tote and a nest of clothes. I put my gloves, my headlamp, and the shovel in the trunk. We picked up Josephine in St. Francisville. She came out the front door as we drove up, carrying a scuffed-up suitcase, a folded map.

When Josephine saw Bordelon in the backseat, she stopped, placed her hand on her own heart.

"I'll be damned," she said. "I didn't know."

"It's just a plus-one," said Bordelon, tapping her stomach.

Then Josephine said nothing, bowed her head for a long time.

I set my phone's GPS to Boulder City. We left—the three of us—in my tomato-red Honda, Josephine in the passenger seat, Bordelon laid out in the back, her bare feet up on the window, her Jackie Os hiding her drowsy, blue-shadowed eyes, her hand over her cantaloupe belly. Josephine, her eyes brimming with fretfulness, looked behind her to Bordelon.

"Poor child," Josephine said. "Looks to me like she's exhausted."

"She sleeps all the time," I said.

I sped past packs of cars on the highway. Josephine gripped the handle above the window.

On the radio, there was Little Richard and Buddy Holly. There was Cash and Parton and Presley and Berry and Domino. The DJ said the station was holding a contest for the fifteenth caller. He rattled off trivia while waiting for calls to come. Presley was born in Tupelo, Mississippi, along with a stillborn twin. Cash's nickname had been The Undertaker. Dolly's middle name was Rebecca.

In Denton, Texas, we stopped for gas. Bordelon went inside for the bathroom, her baby-holding hips moving side to side as she walked. Josephine swiped her credit card at the pump but got right back in the car, didn't move from the seat while I pumped the gas. Bordelon came out of the station with a tube of BBQ Pringles, three cans of ginger ale, a Powerball ticket.

"They've got hot sandwiches in there," she said. "Roast beef and onions."

"Have what you want," I said.

"I don't know," she said. "I might be sick. You want me to vomit roast beef and onions?"

I pointed to the ticket. "Looks like you're feeling lucky."

"I figured if there was a good time," she said, "now is it. Beatrice and I used to get scratch-offs every week. We'd sit down and eat popcorn and start scratching everything off."

"How'd you do?"

"About even," she said. "Beatrice went for Bingo every Thursday."

"How'd she do?"

"About even."

"We can get popcorn."

"I'll just get sad," she said. "You want me sad? And vomiting roast beef and onions?"

In Lubbock, a dinky red truck stood parked on the shoulder. A man sat in the truck bed, surrounded by potted plants of all sizes and a sign: FOR SALE. PAY WHAT YOU WILL.

I pulled off and stopped. Bordelon stayed asleep in the back while Josephine and I got out. Josephine inspected each one, running her fingertips along the leaves. She chose one of the simpler plants, a tiny potted fern, barely alive. The brown leaves were chewed up and brittle, striped and spotted with white. It looked lonely, in need of a good home.

Did he take credit cards? she asked him. Yes, he said, he took credit cards. He had a frosty beard and white hair sprouting from his ears.

"This is a blue star fern?" Josephine said.

"That's right," he said. "*Phlebodium aureum.*"

"*Phlebod—*" Josephine tried to repeat it.

"*Phlebodium aureum,*" he said again. "I used to teach this stuff. High school biology. I'd bring plants into the classroom, line them up, write their scientific names on the board."

"How much water does a blue star take?" I said.

"Just give her lots of shade," he said.

"Her?"

He tapped the plant. "Give her shade. Ferns like the dark."

"Biology," said Josephine. "I'm guessing you taught ninth grade. I was a teacher too."

"What county?" he said.

"Not here."

"Well, I don't teach anymore," he said. "I got out. My wife just died. Happened fast."

"I'm sorry."

"She lived long but died quick. They took her away just a month ago. I brought all her things out to the yard and burned them up too, everything. Her clothes, her books, burned it all up. Didn't seem right for her things to outlive her."

"God be with you," Josephine said.

"God is fire," he said. "Fire is God. Fire purifies the soul."

Then he was back to talking about plants. He was cursed with knowledge and could teach it to no one. He pointed to every plant in his truck bed and told us the name of each. Josephine knew the names of some too. It was as if the plants were his children, and he was their namer. Wood fern. *Thelypteris kunthii.* Spiderwort and phlox. Snakeroot, buttonwillow, jessamine.

* * *

It seemed that Texas would not stop. We passed farmland, fields of grazing longhorns, shotgun homes, palace homes, a barn split in two by a storm. We stayed the night at the Honey Cactus Inn an hour outside of Denton. Only a few lonesome cars in the lot. At the front desk, the girl checking us in took a look at Bordelon's swelled-up belly and swelled-up feet and gave us a large room for a quarter of the price. We had two beds and a pullout sofa. Josephine made Bordelon lie down first thing, removed her flip-flops, put up her feet on two thin pillows, gave her that helpless, brimming look.

"You poor, poor child," she said.

I slept on the pullout, feeling the coils dig into my back through the night. I kept my duffel with my mother's urn next to me, even cozied the blankets around it. Bordelon and Josephine slept in their separate twin beds through the morning, Bordelon's stomach rising and falling with her gut-deep snores. I went to the bathroom and looked at my tired self. My greasy hair, my eyes small and swollen. Bordelon's Jackie Os sat by the sink, just staring up at me, next to her sparkling tube of Wet n Wild. I—quietly, gently—turned the bolt to lock the bathroom door. Then I put on her sunglasses, sucked in my cheeks, looked right in the mirror. I opened the lip gloss and smoothly ran the applicator along my skinny lips. I stared in the mirror a long time. I didn't have such a bad-looking face, but I could never look as good as Bordelon. I stared and stared at myself, longer than I ever thought I could.

*   *   *

Texas had no end. We were driving farther and faster from what I knew to be home. Bordelon slept in the back on top of pillows we'd stolen from Honey Cactus. I tuned the radio to '50s and '60s music. The Four Tops were singing "I Can't Help Myself," then Lesley Gore started up with "It's My Party."

Then a commercial. I changed the station and came to church music. I listened and kept it there. *As the deer longs for flowing streams of water, so my soul longs for you, O God. When will I see the face of God? My tears have been my bread.*

"My mother's favorite," I told Josephine.

"Turn it up," she said.

I decided we wouldn't stop that night. I'd drive into the next day. Josephine held the blue star fern in her lap, kept my duffel between her feet. We talked for long stretches of time, punctuated by silence. We came into a rhythm, an understanding. We talked about the clouds in the shapes of gigantic anvils, rain up ahead, feeling alone, my poems, her garden, how her vegetables would die soon, how the blue star fern looked, how the blue star fern felt like a person sitting there with us. We talked about Josephine's mother. She'd died twenty years ago. She'd been cremated—her own decision, not mandated at that time.

"It was her choice," said Josephine. "It didn't upset me. I didn't mind it. But at least my mother had a choice."

"Everyone should have a choice," I said. I looked to sleeping Bordelon in the backseat, a dog-eared *Us Weekly* balanced on her chest.

"I believe that too," said Josephine. "I believe your mother should have had the choice."

"What about Bordelon?" I said. "You think she should have had a choice with the baby?"

"Believe it or not, legally, I do," said Josephine. "Sometimes I'm just a no-good Catholic."

"I get it."

"Naomi," said Josephine, "is a nice name."

"It's my middle name," I lied, only because I'd always wanted it to be. "Alma Naomi."

"That's a mouthful," she said. "Still pretty, though."

"It's not really my middle name," I said. "It's Lee. Alma Lee."

"So you've got many names."

In the condensation on her window, Josephine wrote something with her fingertip. I couldn't see what it was at first. She took her time. When she was done, she leaned back and showed me.

Alma Naomi Lee

We reached New Mexico in the rain. No cars ahead, no cars behind us. I drove slowly this time. Josephine had a prayer against rain, against storms.

> *"Lord, I speak to you*
> *Quiet all winds, all rain*
> *Keep us close, O Lord*
> *Quiet all clouds"*

Bordelon woke, said her back was sore, her legs were sore, her feet felt like footballs. She needed to walk around.

"A New Mexico storm can't be that bad," she said.

But she was wrong. The rain didn't stop, a constant pelting, pounding, bleating companion.

"Fuck. Pull over," said Bordelon. "Pull off the road."

"A little more," I said.

But I wouldn't pull off. I'd told myself I'd drive through the night, and that was what I did, driving straight through, making a dent through the rain in the world.

"Alma, I can't take much more," said Bordelon.

Josephine looked back to her, gave her that brimming look. "You poor child," she said. "We'll make it through. You go to sleep and we'll be there."

"I can't sleep."

"Nevertheless," said Josephine, then started to pray again.

"Quiet all winds, all rain
Quiet all clouds"

The storm wasn't quiet. It squalled and swelled, and I drove.

In Nevada the sun shone like a god. The sky was cloudless, so blue and crystal it was nearly as light as the moon. I'd never seen such an unweathered sky. Mountains rose in the distance. They were like beautiful pyramids. Stone I could not touch.

We drove through Boulder City, a town with an ice-cream shop, an all-night diner, antique stores, a corner market. Families walked up and down the sidewalks, sat outside at a candy store. Parents talked to each other while their kids skipped along the sidewalk. I realized it was Saturday. Bordelon was sitting up in the back, watching everything. Dean Martin's "You're Nobody 'Til Somebody Loves You" played on the radio.

"Keep going," said Josephine. She'd clipped back her hair, put on her Tabasco cap. She'd taken out her map, a real honest-to-goodness paper map, and was running her finger along a crease. "I'll tell you when to turn."

After a while, outside of town, the road became narrow and dusty.

"Keep on, keep going."

In a minute the road turned to gravel. On all sides was flat desert ground, like hard plates. My car skidded, bumped, careened. Josephine gripped the handle.

"Goddamn," said Bordelon. "Slow the fuck down, Alma. I'm going to pee on the seat."

We jumped over a pothole. I decelerated to barely going at all. The mountains seemed farther away. All around us was that cloudless sky and nothing, nothing, except for a patch of alien desert wildflowers here and there, yellow bulbs drooping in the heat.

"Here," said Josephine. *"Here."*

"What do you mean, here?" I said.

"Stop here."

"Pull over?"

"Just stop the car."

I stopped, right in the middle of the road, which was now barely a road. The three of us got out of the car. A hot desert wind—my skin already felt chapped and wind-worn. Bordelon squeezed the muscles along her legs. Josephine visored her face with her hand, looked out to the nothing.

"Where's the graveyard?" I said.

"The map says this is it," said Josephine.

"What do you mean, this is *it*?" said Bordelon. "This is nowhere."

"Didn't Father Malcolm tell you what it would look like?" I said.

Josephine let her eyes trace the horizon, tapped her finger to her chin.

"What I think—" said Josephine. "What I think is that people are buried here."

"Where the hell are they buried?" said Bordelon. She walked out ahead of us a little way, looked to her right, looked to her left.

"All through here," said Josephine. "We can't see them."

"Bodies?" I said.

"Bodies," said Josephine. "And urns. Like yours."

I looked for signs of burial, anything to mark a spot. All I saw were clusters of wildflowers bursting from the desert earth, some like straw, others bright and blooming against the desert's muted colors.

I realized that all through the drive I'd hoped for something we didn't find. I had imagined something particular for my mother without knowing I'd imagined it. If I'd been able to bury my mother the way I'd wished—the grave would be under a tree, plain and unadorned, at the end of a stony path. A headstone in the shape of a small door, rising from the earth. The graveyard would be small, out of the way, deep in a corner of the world. A corner only a few people cared about, one of those people being me.

"This isn't it," I said. "Not here. This isn't the place."

"We came all this way," said Bordelon.

"Not this," I said. "Not this place. Even if we could dig here. Not this." I could feel my eyes begin to itch—the tears might release if I let them. But then the grainy wind picked up, and tears weren't coming.

"Then where?" said Bordelon.

"We have to go back to my yard."

"You couldn't dig."

"I will," I said. "I'll figure it out."

"How?"

"I have to."

"I can help," said Josephine. She was still looking out to the desert, to the sky, visoring her eyes with her hand. She was lost somewhere, looking out that way.

"But we drove all the way here," said Bordelon. "We came just for this."

"But we did get something," said Josephine, looking far to the mountains. "We got to see the desert. Look. Look at the desert."

Bordelon and I walked for a while, fingering wildflower petals, poking at the earth, but Josephine kept looking to the mountains, as if a door might appear.

At the Water

Moonlight paled the highway, its surface like paper. In a half hour we'd made it to I-80. Bordelon fell asleep with her feet up on the window, the Honey Cactus Inn pillows beneath her knees. Josephine turned on the radio. Sinatra sang about luck and ladies. The desert stretched like a stark sea.

In twenty minutes I was pulling into a spot at the Good-Night Motel outside of Boulder City. I waited in the car with sleeping Bordelon in the back. Josephine went inside to get us a room, came out carrying a receipt and a key attached to a key chain with a laminated playing card. Jack of Clubs.

"I can give you something," I told her. Meaning money, meaning something small for the night's stay.

"Don't you think about that," she said.

The GoodNight Motel was the outdoor kind. Doors to the rooms faced the parking lot, half full at ten p.m. Josephine woke Bordelon and helped her out of the car, pushing her dress back down over her stomach. Room 114 was deliciously cold, with a large AC floor unit cranking. Wallpaper peeled off in long scabs. The closet smelled of mold. There were two queen beds made up with lumpy floral bedspreads, a particleboard table between them, with a digital clock, a grubby telephone. A table with a TV and a long, greasy mirror behind it.

Josephine gently set our blue star fern on the table between the beds, spoke quietly to it. "This is home for the night," she said.

Bordelon said this was her second time ever staying in a hotel.

"When was the first?" I said.

"With you!" she said. "In Texas the other night."

"That was your first time ever?"

"Ever."

I'd stayed in a hotel twice—once on a field trip to an aquarium in Florida, another time when my mother and I had driven to Texas one summer just for the hell of it. She'd wanted to see the Alamo.

"Watch this," I said to Bordelon.

I went to the table between the beds, opened the drawer. There it was—a hardback, avocado-colored Bible.

Bordelon picked it up. "For what?" she said.

"For your soul," said Josephine.

"My soul's fine where it is."

"They've got breakfast here," said Josephine.

"In this place?" I said.

"That's what the man at check-in told me," she said.

Bordelon lay down on the bed closest to the window, toed off her flip-flops. The thin carpet, worn down in places to patches of concrete underneath, had stains from water damage. I wouldn't walk barefoot just yet.

"We'll have to be two in one bed," I said.

"The poor child should have her own," Josephine said, looking to Bordelon, who'd already closed her eyes, started packing off to dream world.

"Just a five-minute nap," said Bordelon.

"You share this one with me," Josephine said to me, tapping the corner of the other bed. "I sleep heavy."

I checked for a safe in the closet. There was none. It wasn't that kind of place. I took the Ale River tote from my duffel, got down on the floor, pushed the tote far under the bed.

"Don't forget it there," said Josephine.

"I would never."

I went to the bathroom, turned on the buzzy fluorescent light. The end of the toilet paper was folded in a triangle. I thought about showing that to Bordelon, a hotel gesture same as the Bible. I was taking comfort in these things, things that did not change. I took a rough white washcloth that was folded up on a rack above the toilet, wet the cloth, and scrubbed the dust from the bottoms of my feet, between my toes, under my arms, between my breasts. My mother would call it a spot bath. I changed into a long jersey shirt and drawstring cotton pants that sagged at my waist.

Bordelon was awake again, ready for the bathroom after me. She shut herself in, let the sink and tub faucet run both at once. Josephine set her purse on the floor by the mirror and dug inside, took out a slender tube, squeezed dollops of pearly lotion over her hands and arms. With brisk circles and swipes, she rubbed it all in.

I was cool and tuckered. I got in the bed and turned on the TV. Watched an infomercial about a vegetable chopper. I fell asleep before Bordelon was out of the bathroom. Halfway through the night, I woke and heard Bordelon's warbling snores. Josephine was asleep, facing the wall, her back to mine. We were like two bodies arranged in the womb. That night I dreamed of thunder and asters and humming and rain.

I woke at seven. Bordelon snored lightly, the covers cocooned around her. Beside me, sleeping Josephine made sounds like a prehistoric beast. I stepped into the bathroom and took a bath in frigid water up to my belly button. I tore the paper wrapper off the thin disk of soap I found on the edge of the tub, skimmed the soap over my body. When I was done, I wrapped myself in two rough towels and sat on the closed toilet and thought a while. I reminded myself where I was. Nevada. Nevada. And my mother—she was in ashes beneath the bed I slept in.

I put on my same jersey shirt and napped and dreamed of her. She came toward me, put her hands on my face. The roof opened up above, rainwater cutting through the light. Sheets of it between us, burying her face. I couldn't see her, couldn't hear her.

* * *

Josephine woke and sat up. I pretended to be asleep but peeked through the sliver of an eye. She held her back as if it was sore, went straight to the bathroom. I heard the pipes rumble, then the shower's cold blast.

I was sitting up in bed when she came out. She was dressed in a clean button-down shirt and dark denim skirt. I brought my hand to my lips, pointed to Bordelon still asleep. Josephine nodded. I could hear her just thinking it: *That poor child.*

"Checkout's at noon," she whispered.

I looked at my phone. Ten a.m. I held up both hands with my fingers up. Ten.

"Let's get breakfast," she said.

"Hell, yes," I whispered.

The breakfast room was just another room in the motel. Muggy like ours, with spongy carpet. A large folding table was laid out with Froot Loops, Rice Krispies, Lucky Charms, toast triangles, pastries wrapped in cellophane, small plastic bottles of orange juice, and cartons of chocolate milk.

"Who knew the little GoodNight Motel would have a feast?" I said.

We heaped food on Styrofoam plates. I took tiny boxes of cereal and Bunny bread toast and a raspberry cheese Danish and two cartons of Kleinpeter chocolate milk and soft butter squares wrapped in foil. There were no chairs, nowhere to eat.

"Look there," said Josephine, pointing out the window. "Let's sit there."

"The parking lot?"

"There," she said. "Look past it."

I couldn't believe it. This cruddy place, beyond the lot, even had a pool.

"Goddamn," I said.

The water was a terrifying green. A small, sun-pinked girl floated by in a pinker flamingo inner tube. A man who looked to be her father was half asleep in a plastic chair perched just by the deep end. Somewhere in my car's glove compartment I had a flamingo keychain, and I wanted to go find it and bring it for the little girl to see.

Josephine and I sat in lounge chairs at a table that had the world's saddest umbrella. A sign said NO DIVING and NO GLASS. Another sign said NO DIVING WHATSOEVER, and another handwritten sign just said DO NOT. I liked that one. Do not.

Josephine hunched over her plate, eating a cinnamon bun, licking the sugar from her fingers. She had a little paper cup of coffee. She'd added whipped cream on top—I'd seen her do it in the room, shy about it—in bright, brainy wisps.

The girl floated by in her flamingo inner tube, watching us. If I were her, I'd be watching too. I winked and waggled my eyebrows. She looked away. I'd never seen such a lonesome kid. She looked as lonesome as I'd been. I remembered being quiet like that, being very good, being somber and slow to smile. What else I remembered: hiding in the V of my mother's legs when strangers spoke to me. Not knowing what to say back when they said hello. But being quiet, I reminded myself, didn't mean the same as being good.

We're the Flamingo Girls! I wanted to shout to the girl, to Josephine, in a sudden feeling of love or simple understanding for her. Sudden feelings of love didn't always make sense to me.

Cicadas held forth, asked for our attention. We were eating in silence and gave it to them. But the little girl was singing a triple-note tune, winding in her flamingo way around the pool. The flamingo was losing air, drooping in the water. It made no sense, I knew, but I felt bad for it. The thing wouldn't last. The girl would grow up.

By the time Josephine finished her second cinnamon bun and I'd drunk all my Kleinpeters, the sleeping man opened his eyes and gathered their things—a cooler, sunglasses, a naked baby doll—and called the little girl to him. She pulled herself from the water, and they were gone, just like that.

"You never wanted kids?" I said. "Don't Catholics want children?"

"Not me," she said. "Just a no-good Catholic. My kids were my students. I had enough kids that way."

"I don't mind them," I said. "I don't want one of my own."

"Frank wanted them," she said. "His own."

I'd wondered when she'd bring him up again. She thumbed the dime-size cross around her neck.

"And?" I said.

"And I didn't," she said. "I don't think he ever got that."

"Well, fuck him," I said. "Fuck that shit clown."

Josephine smirked to herself, took a drink of her whipped cream coffee.

"You can say it," I said. "You can say fuck him."

She took her mouth from her cup and spoke quietly.
"Fuck that clown," she said.

"There you go."

"Fuck that motherfucking shit fuck," she said a little
louder. "Mother fuck."

I put my hands to the sky. "Hallelujah!" I shouted.
"Amen."

We sat for a minute, looking at the surface of the pool,
calm and dirty, without a ripple.

"I'm going in," I said.

"In the pool?" said Josephine.

"Come on. You too."

"We don't have any towels. Or suits."

"Who cares?"

I didn't think about it anymore. I walked to the pool's
lip and sank a foot in the water. Warm and thick, slimy.

"Feels good to me," I lied.

"It's filthy," Josephine said behind me.

I didn't wait—I jumped, throwing my whole self in,
plunging to the bottom, my feet finding the scabbed floor.
I stayed under, cloaked in the water's warmth, the pool as
large as an emperor's tomb.

Then I rose, my body wanting to float. I looked up
through the surface of the water. Josephine stood at the
pool's edge, waiting. And then she jumped. All at once,
she was beside me, underwater, her gray hair undulating,
her eyes open, her arms and legs weightless. The scars
that circled her mouth, the scars from Frank's cigarettes,
caught the light. They glistened. I imagined the scars not

as wounds. I imagined them as gills. I imagined her long skirt fanning into a tail.

I brought my head up from the murky water into the sun, took a large gulp of air. But I didn't wait. I plunged back beneath with Josephine, opened my mouth underwater. We were on a new planet. I had never felt so alive.

Then I let out a scream, silent in the water.

And Josephine, beside me, opened her mouth and screamed. Long and silent. A thick stream of droplets rushed from both our mouths. We screamed into the water, into the planet. Not out of fear or pain. It was a release. It was a letting go.

Side by side, Josephine and I screamed soundlessly, my whole body caught in a lung-aching scream, an eye-numbing scream. Our sky was the water's surface. Our air was the water, the water rippled and vibrated. My whole body shook, in pulses, in waves, opening.

THREE

Bordelon was awake and laid out in the bed like a sphinx. Her face was fixed, her eyes loaded in a particular way. I could sense she had something to tell us.

"You're soaked," she said. "It's not even raining yet."

"We took a dip," I said.

Josephine went to the bathroom, brought out a couple of thin towels, still wet from our showers, gave one to me. She began to wrap her hair up in the other.

"Are you hungry?" I asked Bordelon.

I'd brought her back a lumpy banana from the breakfast room. She grabbed it from me, pierced the peel with her nail, unclothed the whole thing down the long seam.

"Checkout's in half an hour," said Josephine.

Bordelon held her naked banana, waiting to take a bite.

"Look," said Bordelon. "I'm not leaving. I can't leave. Not today."

"What do you mean you're not leaving?" I said. "We're all leaving."

"Can't yet," she said. "I need to stay still, keep my body still. I can't explain it." She looked to Josephine, hoping. "I can't shove myself back in that car."

"If we start back now," I said. "If I drive through the night, I could try to make it in two days."

"That's two whole days," she said.

"Listen to me," Josephine said. She sat down next to Bordelon on the bed. "You'll be more comfortable in a real place, a real bed."

"My body's telling me something," said Bordelon. "*Don't move. Stay put.*" She crossed her arms over her stomach. "I'm serious," she said. "Please. Not today."

"It costs money," I said. "We can't just stay here."

"I'll pay for it," said Bordelon.

"How?"

"I can't get in that car."

I looked to Josephine.

"Tonight, we can stay," said Josephine. She gave Bordelon that brimming look. "You poor child. You sweet child."

She took pillows from the bed we'd slept in and put them under Bordelon's feet.

"How's that?" said Josephine.

"Better," said Bordelon, lying back, digging her heels into the pillows. At last she took a bite of her banana. "So much better."

"I'll bring you some ice," said Josephine.

"There's no ice maker," I said. "I looked."

"I'll find some."

"I can give you money," Bordelon said to Josephine. "For the room."

"Don't you worry about that."

Bordelon looked down, chewed softly through the banana.

"I'm so hungry," she said.

"I'll go get more," I said.

"Not this," she said. "I need real food. I need grease."

I said I knew just the thing. I said I'd be back in twenty minutes.

I changed into dry clothes and left the room. Josephine had gone in search of ice. I got in my car and drove to a cluster of gas stations and fast-food places I'd seen right off the highway. Cacti sprang up like wild crowns in the vastness of desert just beyond. The ground was the color of clay.

I gassed up at the Texaco, went inside. It was large, with groceries and trinkets and fuzzy dice key chains and Vegas shot glasses. Postcards with pictures of the Rat Pack, David Copperfield, the Bellagio, *What Happens in Vegas*. I thumbed through the racks, thought I might send a postcard to my mother. It took me a full second to remember.

I left the postcards, bought a tube of Vaseline for Josephine, a cheap set of plastic yellow bracelets, a box of Fruit Roll-Ups, a *Star* and *Us Weekly* for Bordelon, a Pounder PBR for me.

At the Wendy's drive-through I ordered fries and Cokes, chili and hamburgers, Frosties and nuggets. The smell of hot fat and oil in my car made me want to devour it all, but I waited. That was something, at least. I had self-control when I wanted.

In the room, they were watching TV, with Josephine rubbing Bordelon's feet. I laid out everything I'd bought on the bed, the food, the magazines, the Vaseline, the bracelets.

"Like Christmas," said Bordelon.

"With french fries," I said.

She hugged me to death with thanks. She lay back with the *Star* and the carton of fries, opened up the Frosty, and started spooning the oozy ice cream into her mouth. Josephine didn't eat. She went to the bathroom and filled a plastic cup at the sink and went to our skeletal blue star fern and watered the spongy soil. I heard her talking to the fern.

"Wake up, little one."

There we were, Bordelon chewing soggy fries on the bed, the AC blasting, the grimy walls, the balding carpet, and something in me leaping with happiness that we were together. I felt bells chime in every cell of my body.

That night, Josephine fell asleep early. The room smelled of fast food and damp air-conditioning. Bordelon and I lay down on her bed among the greasy boxes. The setting sun through the blinds made slats of mauve across her face. She put on the stack of plastic yellow bracelets. On her, they were like gold. She stretched out on her back, took up her hair with one hand, pinched it and twisted it around and around at the back of her head and held it there, and then let the whole dark mane flood down her back like oil. I looked to the other bed, made sure Josephine was turned to the wall and snoring. I opened my Pounder and held it out to Bordelon.

"Here."

"What?" she said.

"You can have my first sip."

She took the can from me, closed her eyes, tilted her head back. I heard the liquid slosh in her mouth, slide down her throat.

"God, it's good," she said. "God."

I took back my drink. We switched on the Home Shopping Network and set it to mute. Bordelon said she liked the impossibly bright colors, clothes being modeled on women of all sizes. She said she liked thinking of a middle-aged woman in Idaho at one o'clock in the morning deciding she'd buy a tunic with a pineapple design for the beach.

Bordelon fell asleep with her mouth open, like a baby. Josephine breathed heavily from the other bed. I went to the window and looked at the cars in the lot. Then I turned and stared at everything we had, all the objects around the room. I was so tired but awake; I felt the room turn and glide. I watched shapes and shadows on the darkened walls, the greasy mirror. It started to lightly rain. Even in the desert it could rain. *Good*, I thought. Thunder. Not too much, but just enough.

We were together. We were three. There was nothing better I could think of. Just us, *here*, *here*, us three.

I woke to the rain pattering at the window. I heard Josephine in the shower, the pipes clanging through the walls. The clock radio read 6:17 a.m. That was when I saw our fern. It was sitting right where Josephine had first placed it, but now—it was glorious and alive. New, glossy leaves spilled up and over the pot, the frond tips reaching, touching the telephone. And tendrils—the soil had sprouted tendrils. I could smell their lushness, their ripe, newborn life. They curlicued down over the pot's edge. Down, down, down, coiled and sleek, an unearthly, alien green.

I wanted to wash my face, throw water over my sleepy eyes, but I stood and stretched instead. I knew the urn would still be there, but I looked all the same—the Ale River tote was right where I'd left it, holding my mother's ashes.

I didn't know how many minutes had passed, but Josephine came out dressed in clean clothes, a towel around her neck. I pointed to the fern.

"I'll be damned," whispered Josephine, her eyes wide.

She sat on the bed and took the end of a tendril in her hand. A wonder. She held the tendril close to her eyes, inspecting, like a botanist or a painter.

We let Bordelon sleep, walked in the rain to the breakfast room, loaded our plates. I took a small box of Kix, two chocolate milks, a wrapped Danish with white icing for Bordelon. She was up when we came back, surrounded by pillows in the bed, her large belly the size of a pumpkin beneath the covers.

"Raining harder now," Bordelon said. "Bet the lights go out. For the whole hotel."

I set cartons of milk by the clock on the table, handed her the Danish. She tore into the cellophane with her teeth.

"It's not storming," I said.

"But it's the desert. They don't know how to deal with these things. Bet the power goes out today. I'll bet you a box of Lucky Charms."

"Put your feet up," said Josephine, taking Bordelon's legs out from under the covers and arranging pillows under her knees. "Come on now. Your ankles look bad." She whistled low. "Damn."

I looked too. They were puffed out and veiny, pricked with red. Her feet were even worse.

"I'm deciding," said Josephine. "We're staying another night."

"Really?" I said.

"I want her to rest," said Josephine. "It's raining too. And I've seen you drive in the rain."

"Thank God," said Bordelon. She threw herself back on the nest of pillows. "Thank God."

Just an hour went by, and she said she was feeling funny.

"How funny?" said Josephine.

"Nothing big, just funny," said Bordelon. She said she wanted to take a bath. With a washcloth I'd scrubbed out the tub, gotten it as clean as I could, but there were still rings of grime around the drain, ropy rust stains under the faucet.

Bordelon disappeared into the bathroom, turned on the water for half an hour. Josephine got into the bed, closed her eyes, soon filling the room with her snores, her blankets tunneled around her. Somehow the blue star fern looked like it had grown even more, covering part of the clock, the base of the lamp. The fern must have liked just where it was. It must have liked things not changing, being in the same place, drinking its water at the same time each day, thinking it had its own normal life. I looked out the window, watched the rain hammer the hoods of parked cars.

A desert wildflower with banana-yellow leaves bloomed in a patch of dirt.

Bordelon came out of the bathroom all sleepy and soft, all listless and warm. She wore a long T-shirt, her hair pulled up, with wet, curly wisps at her ears. She got into the bed.

"Don't forget these," I said. I went to the bed's edge, pulled the pillows beneath her feet.

She closed her eyes. "I bet the power's going out," she said, almost asleep. "They don't know shit about rain in the desert. Rain'll shut down the town."

"Try to sleep," I said.

"Alma," she said. "Where are you going to bury Naomi?"

"I told you."

"You couldn't dig up your own yard. I *told* you, it's a sign."

"Go to sleep," I said.

I pulled on jeans, my pair of canary Keds, let Josephine and Bordelon sleep. I shut the door gently, walked outside to my car. The muted sky rained on. Far off, a bird sang a two-note song. One note high, the other low, one short, one long. The lyric lilt, ho-hum, see-saw. The sound came nearer as I walked.

I drove in the rain to the Texaco with the Shirelles on the radio. I bought Donettes and Uno cards and pizza slices, a Red Stripe six-pack. I was eating up my credit, and so be it. On the radio news on the drive back I heard that it happened—the Senate had voted that funerals, any gatherings of mourning, would be made illegal. And there was more. Bodies in some public graveyards were going to be claimed by the government. Bodies buried years ago would be dug up and cremated. The land would be sold for profit.

When I came into the room, Bordelon and Josephine were awake, watching the TV from their own beds. Bordelon said she was feeling more herself now.

"Must have been just one of those things," she said.

"We'll see how it goes in the morning," said Josephine.

I brought out my presents, the food, the Uno cards. Josephine said she wasn't hungry. It was all for me and Bordelon. I got into bed with Bordelon, handed her a slice. While we ate pizza in the bed, I said, "Let's play." Bordelon said she knew the game. I dealt two hands. We dealt and stacked and drew and let ourselves go wild with Draw Fours and Reverses and Skips, the cards greasy from our pizza hands. Josephine watched us from the other bed, clapping when one of us made a good trick.

We let ourselves be loud. We turned our volume up. I played each of my cards with a crash, shouting, "Draw! Draw! Draw!"

I showed them how I could open beer bottles with my teeth. The caps went flying. I lunged after them like a springing cat.

That night, we were happy. I could have relived it over and over. Hopped up on Red Stripe, I jumped on the bed and cooed out a yell and started to sing "It's My Party."

Bordelon whooped and sang along. Josephine erupted in low trills of laughter, drank half a Red Stripe, clapped her hands along as I sang off-key.

Later, I dreamed that the blue star fern grew up and out, over our heads, over our beds, crawled up the walls, up to the ceiling, grew into a dense thicket, hiding us, guarding us, covering every corner of our pitiful room.

ANOTHER LIFE

On the third morning, Bordelon said her insides were leaping.

"What does that mean?" said Josephine.

"The baby's dancing, maybe, I don't know," said Bordelon. "I had too much sugar. I don't know, I don't know."

A half hour later, she said the baby still danced inside her.

"Roll over," Josephine said. "Lie down on your side."

"What will that do?"

"Maybe something," said Josephine.

I walked down to the ice machine. Josephine had found one outside. It was 8:30, still raining. I saw a family of four packing up and getting into a van, a small, sleepy boy wearing red pajamas and Mickey Mouse ears.

In the room, Bordelon lay on her side like a beached mermaid. Josephine was behind her on the bed, rubbing her back. I brought a cup of ice to Bordelon. She took a handful, put the whole pile in her mouth, and sucked.

"It's raining," I said.

"The power's going out," said Bordelon. "They don't know how to do it in the desert."

"Do what?"

"Have rain."

Five minutes later she was groaning. Josephine rubbed her neck in circles with the flat of her hand.

"Tell me where it's hurting," she said.

"Inside," said Bordelon. "I don't know." She groaned out again. "Shit, fuck," she said.

"Where?" said Josephine.

"Everywhere," said Bordelon. "I don't know."

"Could be the pizza," I said. "Just indigestion."

"Sit up for me," Josephine said to her.

Bordelon squeezed her eyes closed. "Shit. Fuck. Fuck."

Josephine put her hands under Bordelon's arms, raised her up on the bed, holding her arms out in the shape of a cross.

"Help me now," said Josephine. "Sit up for me."

"I can't," said Bordelon, not even opening her eyes. "I can't."

"Give her more ice," Josephine said to me.

I took out a thick piece, put it inside her mouth. Bordelon moved it around with her tongue, the ice scrabbling around her teeth. Five minutes later, and she was groaning more.

"Okay," said Josephine. "I'm deciding. We're going to go."

Bordelon opened her eyes. "Go where? I'm not moving."

"To the hospital."

Josephine was still holding Bordelon under her arms, like that was going to help something. What did I know? Maybe it did.

"It's not time for that," said Bordelon. "I've got two more months."

"Nevertheless," said Josephine.

She told me to take out my phone, find the nearest hospital.

"She doesn't have insurance," I said. "If we can get to Louisiana—"

"Alma," said Josephine. "We're going today. This morning. You can't fool with these things."

Josephine sat in the backseat, with Bordelon laid out, holding on to her paisley purse, her feet up on Josephine's lap. I was frantic. At every light I tapped the window in a delirious rhythm. I put on the Carpenters. I drove down the morning streets, the rain seeming to follow us, pecking and biting at my windshield, the roof of my car. The Carpenters sang us through. Josephine had told me to pack Bordelon a bag. I stuffed my duffel with a change of clothes, Bordelon's toothbrush and magazines. Just before we left, I went under the bed and snatched the Ale River tote with my mother's urn. I wasn't going to leave my mother by herself.

In the rearview, I saw Bordelon change positions. She lay down, her face, with eyes closed, pressed into Josephine's chest, with Josephine's hand on her head.

Halfway there, she said, "The power's going out, and we'll be sitting there in the dark with the nurses rushing around, the doctors losing their shit."

"They've got generators," said Josephine. "Every hospital has one. Sit back now."

Three-quarters of the way there, Bordelon said, "Shit. Fuck. Fuck."

"Shit. Fuck. Fuck," I chanted with her.

"Just relax now," said Josephine.

"Shit, fuck, fuck!" I said. "Shit, fuck, fuck."

Bordelon yelled out in pain. "Shit, fuck, fuck!" I chanted with her.

"Shit. Fuck. Fuck! Shit. Fuck. Fuck!"

"All right now," said Josephine. "All right."

When we came to Kindred Valley Hospital, the rain picked up to a thrash. My tires skidded on the circular road.

"Alma," said Josephine. "I swear."

"We're here," I said. "We're already here."

"Drive to Emergency. They'll have a drop-off."

I followed the signs labeled in red, drove up a thin, windy road, stopped in front of the sliding glass doors. Emergency.

"Come on, sweet girl," Josephine said.

She helped Bordelon out of the car. Bordelon was holding her stomach, scuffling out in those pink, sparkling flip-flops I'd first met her in.

"When the lights go out," said Bordelon, "remember who said it."

"I'll wait right here," I said.

"No. You park and come in," said Josephine.

I watched them walk up to the doors, Josephine helping Bordelon balance through her pain and the rain.

When Bordelon gave birth, she was not lost to the stars.

I sat beside Josephine in the waiting room. She picked up a *Newsweek* from the table while I stayed in my thoughts, wondering how much money I could put on my credit card. A doctor came out, told us the news. The baby was five and a half pounds, taking oxygen in the NICU, was breathing, would be okay, yes, would be okay. The baby would need to stay there a few days. Bordelon was doing just fine. Bordelon was resting. I was so relieved, I thought my heart would rise and come up through my head.

The power stayed on. The rain slowed. We waited the whole rest of the morning. We read magazines in silence, waiting for the doctor again.

Finally Josephine said, "You go back to the motel. Get some rest. I'll wait here."

"You need rest too."

"Me?" said Josephine. "I could last here all night."

I drove back to GoodNight. I told myself I would take a bath, watch some TV, lie down, and let the drizzling rain lull me. Really what I did when I got in the room was lock the bathroom door and sit on the edge of the tub and hold my head in my hands.

When I came out of the bathroom, I checked the time on the clock radio, and there was the fern. It had grown again, the fronds fuller, spilling out over half the table. They were a smooth, deep green, greener-than-emerald green. A few tendrils reached the floor, curling at their ends like treble clefs. It looked like it needed nothing in the world, except for us. It was as alive as I was, as alive as anything living I'd ever seen.

January

In the crisp bone of night, we drove. The moon was so close it seemed to follow. With me were Josephine, Pegeen, Bordelon, and the baby, Beatrice, eight weeks old, whimpering and cooing in the back, fastened in her car seat. Josephine sat on the passenger side, held the blue star fern in her lap. Moonlight hit the Pearl-Eye Picture of my mother that I'd taped on my dash in memoriam.

And here, in my lap while I drove, was the tote bag with my mother's urn.

We'd brought our long spades and gloves, a lantern, a thermos of water, a bottle of whiskey. We were ready to work.

We arrived at the crepe myrtle, blooming just as brightly in the night. We walked to it quietly, Josephine carrying the shovels like they were spears. Bordelon had the lanterns, Pegeen had the whiskey. I carried Beatrice, her silky head on my shoulder. The branches of fuchsia pointed moonward.

Just beneath the tree's branches, Josephine, Pegeen, and I took up the shovels. We broke the earth and dug. Bordelon sat on the wet ground, holding wide-eyed Beatrice. They watched the long arms of our shovels, our arcing swoops, the earth smooth as it came up.

Bordelon and Beatrice were living with me, and I'd have them for as long as they'd stay. What I hoped was they'd never leave.

The myrtle's leaves shook with the wind. In the quiet of an hour, we'd made a large hole. I unwrapped the urn and laid it inside. The metal glowed like a meteor in the ground.

We covered the spot with earth and stood for a minute. Pegeen looked to the sky. Bordelon stood too, with Beatrice, sleeping now, in her arms. Josephine bowed her head. In the lantern light I saw her mouth words. I could not tell what she said. I said my own words in my head. *Rest well, soul. Rest.* When Josephine raised her head, she began to sing. A voice clear and high, with brawn and booming force. *"As the deer longs for flowing streams of water, so my soul longs for you, O God."* My mother would have sung with her. The notes were long and lingering.

I removed the blue star fern from its pot and planted it at the place where we'd buried the urn, let the tendrils flow over the ground. Then I sat and cried for my mother, for her life and her body. I cried so much I felt my eyes swell and heave. Every cell in my body lit up. I felt my eyes as moons, as radiant disks, and everything in me, alive, singing mournfully.

I opened the whiskey. Bordelon, Josephine, Pegeen, and I passed around the bottle while we let Beatrice sleep, while we watched the myrtle and the moon, shining above the fern that marked the place. I knew where my mother was.

ACKNOWLEDGMENTS

I am wholeheartedly grateful to you—

Katie Raissian and everyone at Grove

Jin Auh, Elizabeth Pratt, and the Wylie Agency

MacDowell, Vermont Studio Center, Djerassi, Tin House

Black Mountain Institute, Rona Jaffe Foundation

my colleagues at the Center for Writers at the University of Southern Mississippi

Corinna Barsan, Mark Richard, Janet Fitch, Emily Setina, Donald Revell, Claudia Keelan

195

Marianne Chan, Colleen O'Brien, Brandon Krieg, Carol Ko, Lee Pinkas, Maegan Poland, Lorinda Toledo, Ernie Wang, Becky Robison, M. O. Walsh, Rachel Hochhauser, Amy Silverberg, Shelly Oria, Kathleen Bogart, Leah Breen Houk, Emily Nemens, Mira Dalju

my father, Tibi

my mother, Marjorie

my brother, Owen

my mother-in-law, Petula

This book is for my daughter, Willa, and my husband, Craig. And for Mary Belle, whom I miss every day.